THE FR
OF SURVIVAL

The second of the
'Fragility' series

A Science Fiction/Apocalyptic novel

By Paul Money

Cover artwork:
Principal Designer ASP

© Paul Money/Astrospace

Shutterstock.com
@ Kamenetskiy Konstantin x3
@ UrmasHaljaste
@ geogif

COPYRIGHT

Astrospace Publications
18 College Park, Horncastle, Lincolnshire LN9 6RE
England/UK
www.astrospace.co.uk

Copyright © Paul Money
August 2023
All rights reserved.

The right of Paul Money to be identified as the author of this work has been asserted by him in accordance with the Copyright, Designs and Patents Act 1988 (UK).

All the characters in the story are fictional and any resemblance to real persons either living or dead is purely coincidental.

No part of this book may be reproduced in any form other than that which it was purchased and without the written permission of the author.

This book is licensed for your personal enjoyment only and may not be re-sold or given away to other people in either this or any other format.

Language: UK English

ACKNOWLEDGEMENTS

The author would like to acknowledge the support and help of his wife, Lorraine, in listening to the idea of the novel, how it developed and giving both invaluable advice, encouragement and editing ideas as the story progressed.

He would also like to thank the following for their advice, informed wisdom, patience and encouragement regarding this novel:

Gill Hart
Julian Onions
Mary McIntyre
Pete Williamson

CONTENTS

The Fragility of Survival

Copyright

Acknowledgements

Preface   1

Prologue   2

In the beginning…   4

Chapter 1: Arrival   5

Chapter 2: The lost caves   14

Chapter 3: Into the depths   22

Chapter 4: Of sunbathers and cavers   33

Chapter 5: In the darkest depths   47

Chapter 6: Down deep inside…   59

Chapter 7: Shock…   68

Chapter 8: Desolation   80

Chapter 9: The wanderers   91

Chapter 10: Of tins and a sleep   99

Chapter 11: Game on…   109

Chapter 12: Back on the 'road' again   118

Chapter 13: Second arrival   128

Chapter 14: Against the odds   139

Chapter 15: Downhill   154

Interlude	164
Earth: 12,000 BC	165
Discovery	172
Chapter 16: What? Where? How?	173
Chapter 17: The meeting	179
Chapter 18: Explanations	186
Chapter 19: Their side of the story	195
Chapter 20: Revelations	205
Chapter 21: Revelations II	214
Chapter 22: A limited future…	221
Epilogue	228
Authors Note	230
Astrospace Fiction Newsletter	232
The last Voyage of the StarVista 4	233
The James Hansone Ghost Mysteries	235
About the Author	236

PREFACE

Two couples on holiday in the Algarve
Scott and Katrina, Danny and Robyn

One couple who likes sunbathing on the beach …
One couple who likes exploring the region …
>A simple two week holiday in the sun.
>What could go wrong?

How about the end of the world as we know it for starters?

A desperate plight for one couple

>An even more desperate plight for the other

>>as they discover ***the fragility of survival…***

PROLOGUE

For some, holidays come but once a year, so are eagerly awaited. You work hard at whatever your job is so that special time away is often the most precious.

So it was for a young-ish foursome who for over a decade had enjoyed travelling to the Algarve in southern Portugal to enjoy the sun, sea, sand and of course sex. OK, not quite the latter as much as they used to do but hey ho, they were married and settled in their ways now.

Or you would think so.

Scott and Katrina lived in Kent whilst Danny and Robyn lived in Swindon, but Scott and Danny had been friends for a long time, since their uni' days in fact. They'd met 'the girls' on a holiday to the Lake District and discovered Katrina worked in London close to where Danny was working as financial consultant.

Inevitably they hooked up, Katrina falling for Scott and Danny for Robyn. Complete opposites when it came to interests, but the bedrooms always won out when it came to being passionate. For Danny and Katrina however, holidays meant getting away from the stress of the city and simply winding down for two weeks in the sun on a golden sandy beach somewhere foreign, namely the Algarve.

After a couple of holidays together, Scott discovered that Robyn was bored stiff of just lying on the beach so when they both suggested exploring the local sights, Katrina had suggested they should do so together if they didn't want to enjoy the fabulous sun-soaked beaches …

…and so it began …

IN THE BEGINNING…

CHAPTER 1: ARRIVAL

"Hello."

The voice echoed down to them as they disembarked from the hire car and the four looked round to see who it was.

"Hello, you must be the Peterson group? Yes?"

The first of the two men out of the car realised the lady was calling out to them and he waved back at her.

"Yes, indeed, we were not sure we had found the right place but it looks like we did after all. I'm Scott Peterson, that's Danny, our wives, Katrina and Robyn. You must be Judith?"

"Ja, everyone calls me Judy and you can too."

Katrina smiled and noted the accent. "German or Austrian?" she asked as Judy began to shake their hands in turn, quite enthusiastically as it happened as Katrina began to wonder if her arm would fall off.

"Yes, sorry, I often drop back into my native tongue, my father was Austrian and my mother was German so you can imagine it was an interesting time growing up. How did you find customs, or should I not ask?"

Katrina shrugged and replied.

"Oh, well it took quite a while but we're here now and that's all that matters. Baggage took the longest but the car hire was excellent, thank you for organising it for us. By the way, I prefer being called Trina for short as I've always liked the sound of it, like a ringing bell."

"Ja, Trina it is, I hope I remember as I have so many guests through the year it can be confuzing unless you become regulars.

Indeed, you are here for holiday in the wonderful Algarve so as you say, kick off die shoes and hav' fun here. We hav' one rule however, we try not to talk politics with our guests, it is the best way."

Danny nodded approval. "Sun sea and sand is what I want and lots of it please."

"You forgot the beer!" chimed in Scott as Trina smiled at Danny, then nodded in agreement at Scott's remark. They grabbed their suitcases out of the boot of the hire car and turned to Judith for directions.

Judy looked at each of the women with a little puzzled expression. "Excuse me but I am not sure, forgive me, who is with who?" Scott chuckled and began to point at the two wives.

"Katrina and I are married whilst Robyn is married to Danny." Trina wrinkled her nose at the use of her full name but said nothing. It was a regular thing and annoying to boot, but no matter what she said, he always forgot.

"Ah, gut, I did not want to be calling the wrong wife with the wrong husband and cause lots of problems, *ha!* Come inside and we can get you booked in; I will show you to your rooms. Would you like some lemonade? It is freshly made from local lemons, the Algarve is famous for its abundance of fruits and vee hav' oranges, lemons, loquats and apricots, all depending on the time of year of course.

Here at our holiday villa, we make lots of homemade foods and if you wish there are some you can buy during your stay for when you take trips out."

Judy stopped next to a doorway and indicated for them to enter. The room was a large lounge like area with a dining room off to one side and steep stairs to the right.

"This is the shared lounge for your stay and if you want any evening meals then please let me know the day before so I can let you have a menu for what I can cook.

I hav' to get the goods in but often have plenty in my kitchen as long as there are no special diets. I am right in thinking there were no special things to take note of?"

"No, we're all meat eaters although Katrina, my love, has been wondering about going vegetarian haven't you dear?"

Trina looked at him as much to say, 'why did you mention that?' and shook her head.

"Don't mind me," she cut in, "I haven't changed yet, although I will say I don't like it when the food looks as it did before being killed so I'm not keen on fish unless it has been processed. Oh, and anything that still has its legs or wings does put me off a bit."

Judy looked on and smiled as she listened,

nodding all the while. "Have you been to the Algarve before?" she asked innocently.

Danny laughed then stopped himself. "Sorry, yes we are regulars but normally stay over in one of the villas near Albufeira. But this year, Scott and Robyn wanted to do something a bit different so here we are. We usually avoid the local restaurants, especially as fish is one of the main foods of the region and you can imagine what Katrina thinks about that, so we usually seek out anywhere that will serve English or English style food."

Judith noted that that he'd said Scott and Robyn almost as if they were the married couple. She didn't comment but did smile inwardly.

"Well, in that case I won't send you off to our local restaurant, its main delicacy is Carapaus Alimados, or to you, skinned horse mackerel. Forgive me but I'm puzzled again as to who is with who, you mentioned Scott and Robyn, but I thought, Trina, you are with Scott?"

The four holiday makers smiled and began to chatter at once before Scott seemed to take over the conversation.

"Trina and I are together, as are Danny and Robyn. However, Danny and Trina don't like driving around exploring the countryside and prefer to sunbathe on the beaches, as they both have very stressful jobs in London's financial district.

Robyn and I on the other hand, enjoy exploring the culture of an area and the lovely scenery so we split up and do our own things when we're here in the Algarve. This time we thought it would be nice to come further inland instead of always being based close to the coast."

Judy looked bemused. "Oh, how interesting. Well, there is plenty to do locally, and there is an excellent taxi service if you need it so you'll find lots of information in your rooms. Talking of which, let me take you out and around to your part of the accommodation so you can settle in and when you are ready, do please come down and I'll get that lemonade ready for you."

Scott waved his arm gently in a sweeping gesture for her to lead on, and they dutifully followed Judy up the steep stairs to their part of the rather extensive villa.

#

Four days into the holiday and they'd settled into their usual routine. Scott dropped Danny and Trina in Lagoa close to their favourite beach then he and Robyn headed off on their adventures. They'd never explored much of the southwestern coastline so had decided it was their goal for this holiday.

Settling in nicely, several more days went by with the same routine but on the eighth day there was an abrupt change in the weather as a storm front rushed in from the Atlantic. The foursome shopped at the local superstore, found a shoe store stuffed with so many shoes, Robyn and Trina were lost in their element. Scott and Danny could only shake their heads wondering how they'd get everything back home considering their baggage allowance.

Hearing that the day's weather would be bad, they'd arranged for Judy to cook the evening meal and it was whilst they were sitting at the table and having a glass or two of Portuguese local rose wine, that Judy asked if they'd done much exploration so far.

"Well, the beach to the west of Portimao has been explored thoroughly, hasn't it Trina?" Danny laughed as he said it and Trina smirked.

"Well," she added, "I think it's called Praia de Alvor but it does seem to stretch a long way and we did wander a long way along it to find a less busy spot before we settled, but it was worth it."

"Oh gut, very good, it is a long beach but where the river Alvor flows out on the other side is Praia do Vale da Lama and it's even longer if you like long walks. There is alzo a large car park at Praia Meia along there too with the beach so plenty of places to go and sunbathe."

Judy wasn't yet sure what to make of the two couples' arrangements but she knew that her guests own affairs were their own and not for her to speculate. She turned to Robyn.

"Did you find the route to Silves interesting, and did you get to see the castle and church as I suggested yesterday?"

"They were brilliant. Parking wasn't easy but

once we'd found a spot not too far from them, it was impressive taking a tour on the castle walls" answered Robyn as Scott nodded eagerly in agreement. They didn't want to upset their host by telling her they had visited the castle at Silves several times in their past explorations, Judy was so helpful and they didn't want to upset her.

"Do you like walking in the hills or do you prefer to travel somewhere and explore then move onto somewhere else?" Judy enquired as politely as she could. Scott nodded in a sort of half and half way.

"We don't mind a bit of walking, does us good. Well Robyn and I that is, these two just love the beach too much and staying put."

"Well now, that's a bit unfair as we did do some waking on that beach as Trina said earlier." interjected Danny, a little more seriously than he intended.

"And we do sometimes come along with you both to a few of the local nature reserves near our homes " added Trina, Robyn smiled and touched her gently on the arm.

"Yes, of course you do, so Scott, don't imply they don't like walking."

Scott knew the opposite was true but didn't want any bad feelings, after all as they were on holiday together. He looked inquisitively at Judy who was making sure she didn't get involved considering a nerve seemed to have been touched.

"Oh, I was only going to suggest that there are

some caves a few valleys over and some of my guests have drawn up maps for anyone who likes to walk in the countryside and enjoy the scenery. You can get into the caves but can't go very far down, otherwise I think they would have been fenced off as dangerous.

I can let you have directions and one of the maps if you wish to explore tomorrow. The storm front is moving through very quickly and should clear before dawn if the local forecast is correct."

Scott beamed, exploration was his 'thing' and the thought of getting to see caves, even small ones, was much too tempting. He looked at Robyn expectantly and she knew what he was thinking and grinned whilst nodding enthusiastically.

"That would be great, thank you Judy, er, Dankeschön." she said, and Judith smiled in appreciation.

"You are velcome and that is indeed correct, well done and thank you for trying. I'll get things sorted for you for breakfast for you two and..." Judy didn't get a chance to finish.

"Err, we'll all go I think. Won't kill us to have a spot of walking and it would make a change if we all did something together, don't you think?" Danny suggested as Trina looked at him a little shocked. She quickly resigned herself to going along with them, even though Scott knew she was not a big fan of walking very far, especially in a foreign land.

Robyn was just a little stunned that for once

her husband, Danny, wanted to do something on holiday that actually included her.

Judy left them to finish off their dessert still wondering if the right person was in each couple…

CHAPTER 2: THE LOST CAVES

"Bloody hellfire! You want us to go up there?" Danny looked shocked as he gazed at the steep hillside and wondered why he'd volunteered himself and Trina to come along. Indeed, Trina had been grumbling for at least a mile and a half, in fact almost as soon as they'd left the villa.

They'd just passed a farmer working on his tractor and his dog had barked at them but the farmer had said something in Portuguese to it and it settled back down looking dejected. The farmer gave them a 'not more tourists' look then quickly looked down at his tractor and busied himself with it.

"Nooo, the path winds its way back and forth gradually going up so it's not steep at all. Well, not according to this map anyway!" offered Scott as Robyn looked back from further up the path.

"What's up now?" she asked a little impatiently, still wondering why the other two had decided to join them on the trek to the caves. Very unlike them indeed, she mused and had to admit she'd have preferred it if they'd gone to the beach like they normally did.

Scott looked at her knowing what she was thinking. "It's OK, Danny thought we were going straight up!"

"Didn't I tell you that my husband can be a

right plonker at times!" Robyn sighed then turned and continued up the stony path. Danny caught up with Scott and nudged him in the ribs.

"Doing this for you two. I'd rather be on the beach improving this tan and I'm sure Trina feels the same, but if I'm truthful you do more of what we want than the other way round so, fair is fair, that's all I'm saying."

Scott looked back at Trina who was always the last one whenever they all did a walk, which was not exactly as often as Danny had implied, Scott thought to himself.

"Hey up Trinny, keep up, don't want to get lost now do you!" Danny grinned but instantly felt the glacial like stare of Katrina fall on him.

"DON'T EVER CALL ME THAT!" she fired back angrily. "I've got blisters, almost twisted my ankle and I've got scratched by a bush already, so don't push it!"

Scott glanced at his wife and was about to say something when he caught her look as she glared at him. Unlike Danny, as her husband, he knew when to keep quiet. Turning, he caught up with Danny who had put a bit of a sprint on, probably to keep ahead of Katrina to avoid her wrath.

"Sometimes it sounds like she's married to you, not me!" Scott joked. Danny just shrugged and sped up to catch up with Robyn who had put a spurt on and impressively, was leaving them for dust.

They steadily made their way up, zigzagging

along, following the path as it meandered up the side of the valley. It took the best part of another hour, but they reached a flatter spot close to the top with several large boulders, ideal for sitting on, so they all took a rest. Robyn swung her rucksack round to her front and rummaged in it, fetching out four plastic cups, then a flask."Orange squash, I thought alcohol wouldn't be a good idea on this trip!" she saw the grimace on Katrina's face who then chuckled and looked up at her.

"That's why we let you be in charge of the refreshments. You keep us safe, fed and watered without any worries, so much better than if I were in charge of them. Sorry for all the moaning, but now look at the view…"

They all looked ahead and round as before them were undulating hills, many with orange and lemon trees covering them. Splashes of colour breaking up the greenery of the trees and the brownish, to almost orange, soil where it was bare and visible. In the distance was a large bridge spanning the valley further down, perhaps a couple of kilometres away.

Scott whisked his bird watching binoculars out and watched the traffic flowing across the bridge for a couple of minutes. Vehicles of all sorts appeared from each side of the valley, crossed, then briefly vanished before appearing further on. The motorway wound its way off into the distance, heading towards Spain in one direction and towards the western coastline then up to Lisbon the other way.

Danny was also looking around at the view and spotted something back down in the distance, along the path they had taken.

"Looks like we're not the only ones doing this today, looks like a couple of walkers using the same route as we did. Wonder if they are friends with Judy?"

Katrina shrugged. "We're not the only daft ones then. You know what they say, only mad dogs and Englishmen!" she said sarcastically.

"Hah! Well, I have Welsh and Irish in me so I don't think that includes me!" retorted Danny.

"Yet, here you are out in the midday sun!" chuckled Katrina as she shook her head in wonderment. "Hey, Robyn, how far back do you think they are? In, say minutes?"

"Oh, they're a long way off, if we stayed here then I'd guess maybe an hour as they haven't reached the turn off from the road yet and they've got the hillside to negotiate too." she replied looking a little quizzically at Trina who just smiled back at her with an innocent air. Scott looked up at the gorgeous blue sky noting a few streaks aiming downwards, slightly reddish, but shook his head not knowing much about meteorology.

They continued to enjoy the view roughly towards the north. Way off in the distance lay the undulating rises of the highest part of the Algarve, Monchique.

"May be the highest part but it's not really

that impressive considering it seems to stretch out along the horizon. Now the steep hills north of the airport always seem much more impressive, especially when the plane flies over them, just off to the side before it banks round for final arrival." Scott said as he looked about, then checked the map.

"Typical of you, find a fault even in this view with blue skies and hardly any clouds, orange and lemon trees, hot weather. I'm sure Judith our hostess would say 'Vunderbar!" offered Robyn who smiled at him as the others nodded and muttered agreement.

"In that case, break time over, time to move on! We're quite close I gather, across the top of this hill then just over a ridge on the other side." Scott retaliated and stood up, slung his rucksack over onto his back and began to head off along the rough path. Sighing, the rest followed.

Even though Robyn was keen, she would have liked a few more minutes as they'd only stopped for five or so minutes as it was.

They caught up with Scott halfway across the relatively flat top of the hill. Indeed, there were signs that at one stage it may well have been cultivated. Now it appeared to be grazed as a few goats scattered off in the distance on hearing the walkers marching across the landscape.

The track seemed to wander around erratically but then Scott realised they'd drifted off the 'official' track, noting that the map had been hand drawn from memory by others who had ventured along that way. Just as the other three were getting impatient, he shouted 'Yes!' and pointed to a fainter path that began to weave its way down on the other side of the hill. He set off and the rest duly followed.

They descended around twenty meters before Scott suddenly punched the air in triumph.

"Here! Found the entrance!"

They joined him on a partly level and wider section of the path with a hole around the height of a person and twice the width with signs that it had been slightly widened for access.

"Just as Judith described it to me. This is it. 'Cavernas Perdidas', the 'lost caves'."

"Well, if they're lost, how did we find them then clever clogs?" asked Katrina a little more sarcastically than she had intended. Scott scowled at her, then smiled.

"They were lost but apparently a few decades ago a local farmer found them when he was looking for some of his goats after a storm. They were found sheltering inside."

"So surely they should really be called 'Cavernas Encontradas'?" added Danny. Scott again looked a little frustrated at the attitude shown now they'd found their destination.

"Look, I didn't name them! Anyhow, if you don't mind, I'd like to see if I can get in and how far they go, who's with me?" He looked about the group to realise that Danny and Katrina were clearing a spot and setting up small portable folding chairs. Katrina saw his bemused look.

"Seriously? You thought me and Danny would want to hide away in a cave away from the sun and miss out on adding to our tans?"

Robyn laughed. "I didn't, as I spotted the collapsible chairs in your rucksacks. So, tell you what, we'll go into the cave and do a bit of exploring then we'll have the picnic when we come back out."

Danny and Katrina nodded eagerly but Scott was looking up at the sky again.

"What's up? You going to get mardy again eh hubby?" asked Katrina.

"Anyone else think the sky looks a little odd?" Scott said slowly, pointing upwards and noting there were several faint purple-reddish vertical but slightly slanted streaks in the sky.

"Nah, it's a clear deep blue day, we're just not used to it when we're back in good old Blighty!" suggested Danny as he finished setting up the two foldable chairs with their small cup holders. He tilted his sun hat to give better shade as he sat down in the left-hand chair.

He patted the other chair and Katrina smiled and settled into it, adjusting her top, opening it up wider to get more of the sun's rays for her tan.

Scott shrugged and, looking at Robyn, nodded towards the entrance. "Must be me then. Going a bit potty." He suddenly remembered something as he delved into his own rucksack. "Oh, Judy gave me this before we left. A wind-up torch just in case our batteries went flat." He then went quiet and leaned over to Robyn, whispering in her ear. "She gave me two so I slipped one into Danny's rucksack." Scott handed the torch over to Robyn.

"That's clever, I like it. Mind you, we've got fresh batteries, I made sure of that when we were at that supermarket the other day so doubt they'll run out that quickly!" She smiled back at him, grabbed her rucksack and together they carefully entered the cave, watching their heads in the process.

Danny adjusted his sun hat and put his polarised sunglasses back on as he looked up at the sky and frowned. "You know, Scott's right, the sky does look a little odd. Those look like the curtain effect of an aurora. But it can't be, you only see them at night and not usually from this latitude either."

"Stop fussing, I'm sure it's nothing. You only got those new fancy sunglasses a few weeks ago and the weather in England has been rubbish so you haven't had much chance to use them until now.

"Anyway, I know several things that will help take your mind off things." She reached into her own rucksack and brought out two cans of lager, handing one to Danny then opened her loose blouse up even more, somewhat revealingly.

"Ooo, I do love you…" said Danny and winked at her…

CHAPTER 3: INTO THE DEPTHS

It was a scramble and as they entered, their eyes struggled with the abrupt change from such a bright blue day to the darkness of the inside of the cave. Some light filtered through from the opening, as their eyes began to adjust. Just enough for them to negotiate the entrance whilst keeping a look out for loose stones and rubble as they made their way inside.

Although the entrance was about a person height, inside the ground dropped away at a shallow angle. The roof also was a little higher than they had expected and after a couple of metres Scott and Robyn found they could stand up easily without worrying about their heads and Robyn turned on her battery powered torch.

"That's a nice surprise, huh, typical!" She swung the beam round to show them the layout as she stopped abruptly at the small pile of rubbish off to one side. She heard Scott sigh.

"It doesn't matter where you go, people are simply so stupid and have a *couldn't care less* attitude. It doesn't take much to take your rubbish home, but I guess down here it is out of sight, so out of mind," he said sadly.

Turning on his torch he looked towards the back of the small cave, but the rock face stopped any progress in that direction. He heard Robyn say something and he turned to his left to see her shining her torch onto a small opening with a lot of loose rubble at its base.

"What about here? Could be a larger opening if we can clear the rubble away? Didn't Judith say something about a small earthquake a month or so ago - that might have done this do you think?" she asked in hope that their explorations could carry on.

"Could be."

"Good, here, give me a hand and we'll see if it's bigger than it looks."

Scott grinned. "You say the nicest things …"

"Cheeky!" came the retort from Robyn.

They scrabbled away for a few minutes and the hole widened with indications it could originally have been larger still. Robyn shone her torch into it and moved it round slightly to see what was inside.

"Not sure, but it does look like there's another cave back there," she offered as she surveyed the tantalising glimpses beyond the opening.

"Tell you what, shall one of us pop back up to the entrance and suggest we may be some time. I'm sure they'll be happy to carry on sunbathing. I did laugh when I spotted their rucksacks had those folded portable chairs stuck in them," Scott suggested as he peered into the hole shining his torch into it for himself.

"Yeah, but to be fair to them they did come along for the walk and did know we'd explore the cave, so I guess good on them for thinking ahead. I'll go back up and let them know.

Robyn didn't really give Scott a chance to suggest otherwise, and she headed back up towards the bright light of the entrance.

She reached it and poked her head outside wincing at how bright and indeed streaky the sky was.

She saw the pair sitting with a can in each hand and she shook her head. Alcohol in the hot sunshine didn't really mix well but she'd given up on telling Danny to be careful. Katrina heard her and looked back over her shoulder.

"What's up? Not deep enough?"

"The opposite, we've found an opening that may lead to something a bit deeper so we may be some time. You two OK out here?" Robyn replied, already knowing what the answer would be.

"Yeah, go on, knock yourselves out, not literally of course, but take your time, we can drink in the sunbeams whilst you both dwell in the dark depths of beyond!" stated Danny as he waved his can in the air.

"OK, but don't get too burnt, we've still got a bit of a walk back after this." Robyn suggested but heard Danny grumble something about mothering him, or was it smothering him? She couldn't tell.

"You carry on Robyn, we'll be all right, promise. Take as much time as you need if you are having fun. Don't disturb any trolls down there though as we might not hear your screams for help!" Katrina called back to her and smiled. Robyn shook her head and sighed.

"See you both later then. Bye!" She disappeared back into the cave as Katrina looked over at Danny and winked. He in turn reached down into his rucksack, rummaged around then brought out the sunscreen lotion and indicted to Katrina.

"Oo, yes indeed, need a bit of protection. Here, here and indeed here." She touched herself provocatively and Danny raised an eyebrow.

"And we can't have that now, can we?" he said…

#

"They OK?" asked Scott as he showed Robyn the progress he'd made whilst she was back up at the entrance.

"What do you think? Of course, they're happy, sun, seats and indeed I spotted a couple of lager cans too so they're in their element. Guess we're in ours… Wow, that's some progress, I'm sure we can both wriggle through that now?"

"Let's make it a bit wider and deeper too just as a precaution, I don't want to get stuck and end up needing their help to get out! I'd never be able to live it down," Scott said as he held out a hand to help her.

"Good point, nor I. They'd never let us forget it!"

With that they both continued to excavate the gap for another fifteen minutes or so until Robyn sat back on her haunches.

"That looks good enough. But I'm thirsty, fancy a sip?" as she shone the torch upwards into Scott's face, he blinked as she reached into her rucksack and pulled out a bottle of water.

"Ouch, yes, we've been at it for a while and it's easy to get carried away." He took the offered small bottle of water, drank a little then capped it off and handed it back.

As he did so Robyn leaned forward and, holding the torch carefully, she pushed forward ending up half in and half out of the hole

Scott heard her say something that was muffled but his mind was somewhat distracted by the view of her rear sticking out of the hole in her tight shorts. He swallowed hard and gently tapped on her back making her back out of the hole.

"Sorry, I couldn't hear you, it was very muffled. What's it like?" he asked innocently as Robyn brushed down her front that was covered in dust from the hole. Scott didn't discourage her.

"It's amazing, looks like a much bigger cave and quite deep. The ground seems to slope away gently for a few meters so I reckon we can get in and maybe even stand up. You game?"

"You bet. Can I g.." He didn't get to ask the question if he could go first as Robyn required no encouragement. She scrambled into the hole again presenting an interesting view which quickly disappeared into the darkness. Scott was about to peer in when suddenly her face appeared back at the holes entrance, startling him.

"You coming or what?" she asked, then disappeared again to leave him room to crawl into the hole.

Scott didn't need to be asked twice and soon joined her before carefully trying to stand up in the new cave. He reached out, grabbing her by the arm and Robyn turned and helped him to his feet. Her torch was on the floor lodged into a small pile of rocks to illuminate the cave as she helped him and they stood close to each other, face to face, silhouetted against the light.

If it had been in a movie, they'd have probably kissed ...

Instead, Robyn turned and swept her hand around the dim vista on display in the weak light of the torch.

"Welcome to my humble palace of darkness!" she laughed, and Scott had to admire her spirit. They were certainly well matched as a couple yet in all things both of them were attracted to opposites. It seemed a good thing they could enjoy these adventures together whilst allowing the other two their time in the sun.

He looked around and smiled along with her.

"Stalactites over there, a couple of feet long so have been around for a while. Oh, look, over there, looks like a vein of quartz."

Robyn went over to it and shook her head. "No, it's calcite instead, look it crumbles easily, quartz wouldn't do that. But that ..," she pointed off to the left, "...looks like amethyst." She walked over, bent a little and studied it as she shone the torch over the small outcropping, enjoying the play of colour reflected and refracted by the crystals.

"We won't be able to get it out but then why should we spoil it for when others come down here?" she asked innocently. Scott had to agree but stayed quiet.

The cave floor sloped gently away from them and the cave widened with the roof staying roughly the same height. His torchlight could only penetrate so far but it seemed like the cave went on further than the light allowed them to see.

A faint smattering of dust wafted down as they both stood and looked on.

"You feel that?" Scott said in a hushed tone.

"You too?"

"Yeah. A very slight tremor?" he offered, now with a little concern in his voice.

"I know this is exciting but, well, perhaps we should go back up to the entrance just in case?" she suggested noting his tone had changed.

"Yes, you go first then," he replied without thinking and Robyn needed no encouragement as she quickly passed back through into the first cave, followed hastily by Scott.

They stood there for a few minutes, listening and trying to detect any further hints of tremors but after a few minutes Scott broke the silence.

"You know what, I've just had a thought. There's the motorway just down the valley from here and I bet it's simply the rumbling when large lorries cross the valley."

Robyn looked thoughtfully around the gloomy cavern with just the bright pool of light at the entrance.

"Come to think of it, if there had been a real tremor then I'm sure the two sunshine addicts out there would have rushed in to call for us to get out. They certainly haven't done that, so perhaps you are right. Go back down?"

"Yeah, but any other signs like that then we get out, OK?"

"Deal." Robyn turned and headed carefully back to the second entrance then stopped as Scott caught up. "You first, time for me to enjoy your butt instead of the other way round. Just don't fart!"

"Cheeky, I don't know what you mean. *And* I never break wind. Not in ladies company anyway."

"Hah! Look who's being cheeky now!" she teased as Scott bent down, got onto his knees and crawled through the second gap. Robyn had to smile at the sight then as he disappeared she followed him into the second, deeper cave.

"So, there's the amethyst you spotted," said Scott as he stood and carefully moved his torch around the cave. "This side looks smoother than that section over there."

"It's quite a jumble of rubble to the right, I'd be wary of stepping on that as it doesn't look safe. Let's keep to this more solid looking rock on the left for as long as we can."

They made their way carefully along the left side of the cave, occasionally ducking their heads when the roof dipped lower. A few sections became steep, and they carefully scrambled down them, sending some loose stones and dirt off ahead of them.

Occasionally a larger stone was sent skidding along and disappeared into the gloom before making a smashing sound suggesting a steep section a bit further along. One even made a splashing sound, perhaps a puddle or even a small stream underground, mused Scott.

They carefully negotiated the steep section, each of them silently wondering if they were doing the right thing. Curiosity drove them on in silence. More quartz and other crystalline extrusions manifested themselves, sparkling as their torches wafted over them.

"Gosh, it really is awesome. You think we might be the first to come down here?" wondered Robyn out loud.

"Could be, I haven't seen any signs of rubbish which sadly seems to accompany people if they do venture into these unknown parts. So, we may be the discoverers of a new cave network. How cool is that, eh?"

"I'm loving the sound of that. How far down do you think we are?" she asked, looking at an impressive patch of crystals.

Scott took a deep breath then exhaled slowly.

"Difficult to tell as I've not really been taking much notice, concentrating on my footing instead. Perhaps twenty, thirty metres at most? Maybe more..."

Unbeknownst to the pair, they had already descended over fifty metres without any equipment, or thoughts of the dangers. They carried on picking their way over a few loose rocks before Scott stopped dramatically and Robyn bumped into him, grunting her disapproval. He swung his torch across the wall in front and slightly to their left and Robyn let out a gasp.

There were faint drawings showing various animals, stick people and even a few of what looked to be stars and a half moon.

It was extraordinary.

Proof that someone, probably neolithic or earlier, had managed to get into the caves and even leave their marks on the rough wall. Robyn fished out her smartphone and framed the view as best she could.

"Watch out, this will be bright as I've turned the flash on," she warned.

Scott closed his eyes and heard her take a few pictures as he noted the faint and brief flash light up the insides of his eyelids. Opening them he saw she was gawping at the pics and he moved in close and looked over her shoulder. In the gloom the screen was pretty bright as his eyes adjusted.

"That's stunning, look at the detail, there's more there than we can see in this dim light.

They're pristine too. We must be the first to see them in thousands of years. This is an epic find. You wait until we get back and tell the others. They'll wish they had been down here with us when we made the discovery of a lifetime!"

Robyn nodded enthusiastically.

"We might be famous! I wonder if this means there is another way in. If you are right about how far down we are then we're still well above the valley floor, so I wonder if we found a different entrance to what the other people had mapped?"

"No, their map suggested the cave entrance they knew of and dew was quite near the top of the hill. Perhaps there is an entrance lower down, but it had caved in so there's no entrance there anymore. In that case our only route is back up where we came. Shall we continue further down to see if there is anything else?"

Scott saw from the look in Robyn's face even in torchlight that she felt it was a daft question.

"OK, let's just be extra careful as we really are in unknown territory! My gut feeling is that we've been going deeper under the hill rather than heading down and towards the valley side so, yes, let's keep going but be extra careful," he concluded.

Robyn pushed past him shining her torch ahead sweeping up and down so they could see the ground but still keep an eye out for any outcrops from the roof that they could catch their heads on.

It felt like they were on a magical tour of the unknown.

CHAPTER 4: OF SUNBATHERS AND CAVERS

"OK, how long do you think we've got before that other couple reach this spot?" Trina looked around at Danny as she adjusted her sun hat and tilted her sunglasses down so she could see him clearly.

"Well, the dynamic duo have now been inside for about twenty minutes, so unless the others sprinted, I reckon at least half hour or so and they'll be on the other side of the valley behind us, so not in view for a while," he replied and looked back at her, smiling at the sight.

Katrina had removed her shorts to reveal her sunbathing bikini she'd had on underneath all the while and now she removed her flimsy top so there was only the bikini left.

"Good, did you bring that beach roll mat, you know the one I mean?" she asked.

"Oh, indeedy I do and it's rolled up in my rucksack. Danny stood up from his collapsible chair and rummaged in his rucksack, proudly pulling out the rolled-up mat. He unrolled it on a flattish spot, kicking a few small rocks and stones away and stood there as Trina got up and walked over to him. She carefully slipped her hand into his shorts from the leg up and explored as his eyes lit up.

"So, what are you waiting for Dannyo ..."

Trina slipped her bikini top off then her briefs as Danny slipped out of his shorts, already excited as Trina gleefully noted. Kissing, they lay down on the mat and began to make passionate love in the hot sun.

#

Tired and indeed hot, they lay there afterwards resting, then dressed in case the mysterious other couple should suddenly surprise them.

Katrina spoke first. "You don't think they suspect do you?"

"Nah, we've been pretty careful and who's to say they aren't up to something? I mean, they're the ones always wanting to go off together exploring. Exploring what? Each other?" Danny laughed as he spoke, yet brushed off the thoughts that his wife and Scott may also be having an affair.

Katrina was not so sure and persisted. "I don't know, there are times when Scott looks at me almost as if he knows and I'm sure Robyn has given me the odd look or two over the last few months before we came out on holiday."

"I think you are just feeling a little guilty. I've never felt those two had eyes for each other and I've not noticed any odd looks my way. Robyn always dotes on me and anyway, let's just say for arguments sake, they did. Why do they keep letting us have so much time together sunbathing?

I mean of all things to let us do, almost as if we were a real couple, that's the last thing I would encourage if I had any suspicions!

On to a different topic, wow, it's hot! How many times is it now we've come on holiday to the Algarve, six, seven years on the trot? I'm sure it's not been this good for all those times." Danny rolled up the mat and stuffed it back into his rucksack, a little clumsily as it didn't fit as well as when he'd packed it back at the holiday cottage.

"We're not used to it, that's all. Put some more lotion on me love and let's get back to catching those precious rays of golden sunshine." Katrina sat back on her chair and made sure the loose-fitting light top was open but that her bikini bra was fastened, just in case the other couple they'd spied from afar were almost with them.

Danny found the suntan lotion and lovingly applied it to her top then as she bent forward he carefully rubbed it into her back.

"There, done. Now me please," he crouched next to her, and Trina set to and rubbed the lotion on his chest then lower down and slipped her hand a little into his shorts and giggled at him as he smiled with glee.

"You tease. Haven't you had enough yet?" he asked then his face changed, and he stood up quickly, brushing her hand away from his groin.

"Hello, you two guarding the cave then?" the woman asked as she and her girlfriend came walking over the crest of the hillside. They had indeed followed the same path the foursome had trodden around an hour or so earlier.

Katrina snickered a little as quietly as she could, knowing how close they had been to being discovered in a compromising position.

"Yes, you could say that. The other couple love exploring so are inside, they say they've found it goes deeper than expected, so we probably won't see them for a while yet. It gives us a chance to top up our tans as we can't be on the beach today." Danny quickly explained. "I'm Daniel and this is Katrina."

"Nice to meet you both, I'm Sammy and this is my partner Gail. I think we're in the cottage further up from you. Judith did say a foursome had arrived. Pity we had not met up sooner, we would have gladly joined your friends and let you two love birds go off to the beach if that's what you preferred."

Katrina swallowed hard at the sound of 'love birds' and wondered if the couple suspected anything.

"That's very kind of you, yes, that would have been nice but it's not bad up here and we do have our porta chairs, so we've managed to get some rays and hoping for some more yet." She hoped that was convincing enough and Sammy looked around, then nodded, to the path as it dropped down out of sight leading away from where they had come from.

"Another time then, we won't go into the cave

as it might startle your friends. We'll carry on as there is an animal and bird life sanctuary about a mile further along just on the other side of the second valley. We'll bid you farewell and happy sunbathing. Don't think it will cloud over but then the sky has looked a bit odd over the last hour or so. Like seeing an aurora but during daytime. Very odd don't you think?" Sammy added.

"Hadn't really noticed." Katrina lied but with that, and without Gail having said a word, both women set off and were quickly out of sight as they dropped down the side of the hill.

After what seemed like an eternity, but was just a few minutes, Danny burst into laughter.

"Odd couple or what? Looks like Sammy wears the trousers don't ya think?"

"Yes dear, a bit like me with you, eh?" Katrina shot back and laughed as Danny grimaced and stuck his tongue out at her. He looked up at the sky and his smiled faded.

"You know, it does seem odd. I'm sure I can see green, purple and even reddish patches coming and going almost in waves ..."

"Don't be silly, you mean like that aurora thingy that Robyn sometimes goes on about and that Sammy just mentioned? You know, when Robyn tries to get us to do a winter trip up the Norwegian Fjords and see the *lights* - not much chance of that, it's too bloody cold." Trina said disdainfully.

"Yeah, I agree although it does look spectacular

in the brochures. Yes, it is like that except I'm seeing it in daytime. I thought it was a night-time occurrence according to what I read a while back. There's straight lines in a few patches coming down from the sky, red and green now."

"So ... what do we do?" asked Katrina hesitantly as she too began to watch and stare at the strange glows in the sky.

"I really don't know. Don't know if it's a natural thing or something more sinister." Danny fished his small binoculars out and began to look out towards Portimao, sweeping back and forth along the coast. "Trina, this is not right. The sea now looks odd too. Bloody hellfire, it's boiling! Ah ..." he caught his breath in a sharp intake. "There's, there's fires breaking out all over the place on the coast. WOW!"

"WHAT?" Katrina was now alarmed.

"That ... that petrol station we use, I can just see it, but it's on fire! The trees, scrub land, they're just bursting into flames and it's approaching us ..."

Katrina started to shake as Danny tried to keep his footing and she looked at him with alarm. "Feel that? Felt like an earthquake! My god! My skin is tingling. GET IN THE CAVE, NOW!" She grabbed Danny by the arm, and he spun round losing balance as Katrina grabbed her rucksack and headed for the cave entrance. Danny staggered; his sun hat came off as he stopped to grab his own rucksack.

Fumbling around to find his hat he could feel his skin crawling and the top of his head turning hot. He began to think his head would explode, grabbed at his hat but missed. Frantically he gave up on it and the rucksack as he dived into the cave with seconds to spare.

The relief was wonderful in the cool darker inside of the cavern but as both of them tried to catch their breath they realised with mounting horror the outside was now a wall of red and orange flames; smoke funnelled in as gusts of wind driven fire burst through the entrance.

The landscape and indeed for all they knew, the Earth ...

was on fire ...

#

"You know if we keep going on down like this then we'll end up in Oz!" Scott chuckled as he said it, but Robyn was not impressed.

"Oh, for heaven's sake, that's almost as old as the earth!" she exclaimed and shook her head. But it was Scott's way of coming out with the obvious jokes that did make her smile.

Often.

They had carried on deeper, engrossed in their newfound caving skills as they admired the ever-increasing numbers of crystal formations on the nearest side of the cave and roof. Indeed, if they peered hard enough into the gloom of the large cavern they were exploring, there were masses of crystal formations way off on the other side too.

Scott shivered and they instinctively searched in their rucksacks, bringing out lightweight, but warmer ,tops and trousers. He turned to face the other way as they pushed their torches into loose stones facing upwards to give them light and with their backs to each other they began to undress. "Glad you suggested bringing something a bit warmer!" he said as he took off his shorts and put the trousers on then waited for a few moments. "You finished?" he asked, and Robyn turned him on the spot to face her.

"Yep, this look OK to you?"

Scott just smiled and nodded, he didn't want to admit it, but she was lovely in whatever she wore but he had to keep his emotions in check. He waved for them to continue onwards and, grabbing the clothes and stuffing them back into the rucksacks, they set off again.

Further down, partly on a slippery slope, which above ground might have made a good funfair ride, they came across a narrowing of the cave which quickly closed down to a small gap.

"Well, looks like we might have finally reached the limit." Scott looked a little dejected at that thought but Robyn looked more carefully at the gap.

"No, look if we can move those three small boulders I reckon there's more to it."

Once again she didn't give up and pushed into the gap using her torch to see what lay beyond. Scott was left to admire the view as he shook his head then heard her gasp.

She backed out and grabbed the nearest boulder and managed to pull it towards her and, with Scott's help, they moved it off to one side. They tackled the remaining two, but before Robyn could dive back in, Scott beat her to it and wriggled through the enlarged gap. She heard him say something and figured it was 'wow'.

Pushing through the small gap she joined him. They stood up on a ledge about a metre wide with a large, and suspiciously looking deep, crevice falling away from them. In front of them the other side of the cave was five to six metres away, so impossible to jump. They were near the top and it tapered to a close on their right-hand side with a sheer wall and nowhere to go.

"I think we really are stuck this time." muttered Robyn but Scott was peering over the edge, much to her concern.

"Actually, it isn't a sheer drop at all. It's like a volcanic intrusion thingy, you know what I mean, you're the amateur geologist here. Like at Giant's Causeway."

"Oh, an igneous intrusion. Basalt columns, like that?"

"Yes, that's it. Looks like the softer rock has been worn away exposing them."

Scott shone his torch downwards and moved

it about then stopped, pointing at one spot. Robyn followed the beam and shook her head.

"No. No further. We're too deep as it is and if anything happened we could be trapped down here. Scott, it's time to go back. Think of what we're going to say about the cave drawings further up. Think of how jealous the other two will be if we become famous."

"To be honest, I reckon they'd expect us to say we all discovered it together as I doubt they'd like to be left out of the limelight…"

Robyn grimaced at the thought the other two would do that but said nothing.

Scott carefully aimed the torch at his face in an upwards angle as he'd seen in a few horror movies, pulled a face and Robyn laughed than lightly smacked him on his arm.

"Daft bugger."

Scott looked around and deep in his heart he knew she was right. They'd done far more than most people would have done without specialist training.

He turned and wriggled back through the gap, quickly followed by Robyn. Moving upwards they soon reached the more level section where there were copious amounts of crystals lining the cave and they sat down on the floor.

"I need a short rest," said Scott and he looked into his rucksack for his bottle of water as Robyn shone her torch helpfully.

They each took a mouthful and their gaze

met, eyes briefly locked onto each other before becoming embarrassed by the lingering stare and they both glanced away. Scott put the bottle back in its place then noticed something.

"There's light in here." he said, puzzled.

"Yes, the crystals fluoresce slightly due to our torchlight," offered Robyn, but Scott shook his head and turned his torch off, plunging them into darkness.

But it wasn't dark ...

"That's odd, they should quickly fade as there is nothing to keep them going," Robyn observed as she looked about and dimly could see Scott gently illuminated in a purplish, faint glow.

The ground moved.

Really moved.

They sat in the torchlight, shocked, as they heard rumblings reverberate through the cave and some fine dust and small rocks fell all around and onto them. Neither said anything as they both began to scramble back the way they had originally come and before long they reached the first small gap they had enlarged to explore the second cave.

Except there was no longer a gap. The roof had collapsed and there had to be tons of rock completely blocking their exit.

Robyn stared open mouthed and frozen to the spot, unable to say or do anything, as she stood in shock at the view before them in the torchlight.

Scott had his smartphone out and was wafting

it around but sat down heavily on the rough cave floor staring at the screen and shaking his head.

"No signal, nothing at all," he said then realised Robyn was just standing staring at the rock fall.

"Robyn, Robyn, ROBYN!" he called, and it shook her out of her frozen state.

"We're ..."

"Trapped, yes, I know.

But Danny and Trina are outside and likely to be safe and you can guarantee they'll be calling the local emergency services. The important thing is that we're alive and luckily not hurt. If we both just try shouting at the top of our voices then they may hear us and know we're at least alive."

Robyn was unusually quiet but was nodding in agreement as she was trying to convince herself Scott was right. She took a deep breath and swung her torch beam around above them studying the cave, then appeared to change her mind.

"OK. This may sound a bit odd and counter intuitive, but I think we shouldn't shout and that we should go back deeper a little into the cave."

Scott looked at her astonished.

"I don't ..."

"Look around, this section has a lot of cracks in the roof of the cave that suggests it could be unsteady and there could be another rock fall, especially if we shout. We don't want to be under it if that happens, if there's another tremor, especially if we cause it by shouting. A bit further down where the crystals are, appeared to be more solid stable ground so although it does sound daft, I think we'll be safer waiting there just in case."

Scott thought for a second or so, but deep inside he knew he could trust her, so nodded; they set off back down deeper into the second cavern. They reached the spot where Robyn looked about and pointed to the flatter part of the cavern floor, noting the crystals were still gently glowing. "Very odd. If it was just absorption of our torch light, then re-emission, then it should have faded, but they are still glowing from when we were last here."

They both settled down on the rock floor, cross legged facing each other. Scott swung his rucksack round to his front loosening the straps to do so and Robyn did the same so they could use them to lean on if they got tired.

Robyn fished her bottle of orange squash out and took a sip, offered it to Scott who did likewise.

"How much have we got between us?" he asked.

They each pulled out any remaining bottles. Scott just had his water bottle, half full, but it was a litre capacity whilst Robyn had her litre water bottle, still three quarters full and the small bottle of orange squash, just over half full.

"Should do us, those miners in, where was it, Chile? They were stuck underground for almost seventy days, and I doubt we'll be down here for any longer than a few hours or so."

Robyn looked at Scott in the torchlight and frowned. "Charming, you know how to cheer me up don't you!"

Scott shrugged then looked about, a puzzled expression on his face. "Is it me or is it getting warmer and brighter in here?"

They looked around and were astonished as the cavern steadily lit up but with a purple and orange glow emanating from the crystals; they could clearly see the whole of their section of the cavern as well as themselves.

"What the ..." they looked around, lost for words for a moment then Robyn noticed something.

"You feel warm and sleepy?"

Scott was about to answer as they slumped into each other, passing out, yet their bodies so linked that their heads were on each other's shoulders, looking downwards and they remained in a sitting position, unconscious.

CHAPTER 5: IN THE DARKEST DEPTHS

All was still and quiet.

Nothing moved and gradually Scott's torch battery gave out. The crystals continued to glow in varying degrees until they eventually fell dark. Dust slowly settled on the unmoving pair. A few small rocks also fell from the cave roof as occasional slight tremors gently shook the region.

Quiet.

Black.

A complete stillness in the cavern.

A larger tremor rattled the cavern and at the original cave entrance some of the rocks blocking it fell away revealing the light of day.

But not the second cavern's entrance.

Sealed, never to reopen.

Silence.

Deep down, a stirring.

A muffled cough, then another, as Scott began to regain consciousness, but something was wrong. He couldn't open his eyes or mouth. He could just about breathe through his nose, but they seemed close to being blocked and a rising panic threatened to overwhelm him. His legs felt as if they were on fire and he couldn't uncross them but, on the brighter side, his arms were free.

One was draped over Robyn as he felt her head leaning into him delicately balanced on his shoulder. As carefully as he could, in the pitch blackness, he used his left hand to try to fumble his way to and then into his rucksack.

There!

The litre bottle of water.

He pulled it out, wincing with the pain from cramp in his muscles, tried to place it next to his cramped right foot then attempted to unscrew the top with just the one hand.

It finally gave way and came unscrewed but he left it capped as he felt up towards his face with his hand. His eyes seemed to be caked as if they were sealed with gunk and he remembered that it was often called 'sleep in the eyes'.

As a rule, this was a normal function to protect the, but it could temporarily seal them and he knew that a little water could soften it up and allow him to wipe it away. He'd had it plenty of times before, but not this bad. It was like his eyelids were glued together.

He couldn't see if his hand was clean and as a precaution wiped it on the inside of his shirt just in case, as the back of his hand felt like it was caked in dust. Almost knocking the bottle over as he felt around, Scott managed to pick it up and push it into his other hand just as Robyn began to stir.

A little trickle into his cupped hand, he splashed his face and carefully rubbed the gunk away. For a few moments he still couldn't open his eyes then, gradually he felt the lids separate.

Darkness. No light from his torch or the

crystals, so the cavern was jet black. He still couldn't open his mouth and he now realised his nose was virtually blocked and all his efforts so far made him acutely conscious that he could hardly breathe. He pushed his tongue against his lips and rubbed a wet finger on the outside of the cracked lips in the hope of easing them open.

Robyn stirred some more; he felt her trying to move her head then realised she too was beginning to realise she couldn't see or talk and barely breathe. His lips suddenly parted, painfully and he felt a trickle of blood so one of them had to have split. It felt like the upper left side lip where it was the most painful. He took a quick sip of water to moisten his throat.

"Robyn, careful. Don't panic, but I've managed to get the water bottle out. Let me try to get some water to your eyes so you can soften and clear away the gunk."

She tried to say something, naturally it was muffled but she did seem to calm down. Scott carefully moved his hand up towards where he thought her head might be and accidentally caught her under her chin bringing a muffled grunt from her in annoyance.

"Sorry, it's dark, there's no light at all and I don't know where my torch is."

She tried to say something, but it was still muffled. Scott managed to wet his hand and carefully felt her face, carefully wiping her eyes. Suddenly her right eyelid opened then her left lid but at this stage in pitch darkness neither could see if the other's eyes were now properly open.

Scott trickled some more water into his free hand and carefully brought it up to where he thought her mouth was and tried to dribble it across her lips. He had an odd idea, slowly leaned into her and found her face with his and slowly matched lips. He didn't kiss but tried sliding his tongue out to prise her lips open and for a moment he thought she was chuckling. Then it worked and she pushed her head back, coughing several times and taking great gulps of air.

"What the hell, Scott!" she exclaimed.

"Err, I was only trying to help!"

She went quiet but he could hear her breathing heavily.

"Sorry Robyn. I wasn't taking a liberty you know. I was genuinely trying to help," he coughed a few times as the air was very dry in the cavern, then he had a brainwave.

"Your torch in your rucksack. Can't find mine so it must have rolled away." He instinctively tried to move but his calves and legs screamed out in pain as he shuffled, trying to ease the pain and numbness. Robyn too yelped in pain.

"Bleeding hell, my legs!! They're on fire. What happened?" she said suddenly.

By now Scott had settled the pain down and felt for her rucksack, touching something soft. Suddenly Robyn struck out at random slapping his hand and arm as she flailed out in the dark.

"Not THERE!" she cried out indignantly. She now found her arms were less painful, so felt in front of her and managed to find the top of the rucksack. Pulling at the cords, it opened, and rummaged inside before, sounding pleased with herself, she pulled the torch out. Fumbling to find the right end in the dark she switched it on.

Nothing.

Dead.

"I, I don't get it. They were new batteries just yesterday when we were down at the local supermarket. Fresh batteries…dead."

"Could have been a bad batch, it happens. But stranger still, how long have we been down here unconscious for us to gunk up like that?"

"No idea, it's scary, why haven't they found us yet? Must have been a few days but it's dead quiet. Nothing, no sound of digging or drilling. Surely they'd carry on until they'd found our bodies if they'd given up on finding us alive?" she said, a quiver in her voice that belied Robyn's usual mask of strength.

Scott had no answer.

Robyn suddenly had a brief thought and struggled to recall it, then started to rummage in her rucksack again. She sounded like she'd found whatever it was and nudged Scott in the ribs, a bit more forcefully than she'd intended.

"Oww! What have I done now?"

"Sorry, just close your eyes and open them slowly when I say, trust me OK?"

Scott grunted acceptance then even with his eyes closed he heard a strange sound of a whirring noise then his vision showed a pinkish glow filtering through his eyelids, and he opened them up instinctively. Then shut them in pain at the blinding light.

"Well, I did say wait until I said to open them!" Robyn proudly moved the wind-up torch around the cave as Scott opened his eyes, wincing but this time he could keep them open.

"Your vision a bit blurry?" Robyn asked.

"Yes."

"Give it a few minutes. Mine is too but that's probably a consequence of them being stuck shut tight for a while. Dribble some more water into them to moisten them up. Let's not use up the water though as we don't know how long we're going to be stuck down here if no one is coming for us."

Robyn shone the torch over themselves and chuckled. "You ought to see yourself, guess I look like it too, but we're covered in dust and fine rocks. How long have we been down here like this? Can't be more than a few days surely as we'd be dehydrated and any longer, more likely dead!"

Scott was following the torch beam as she waved it around the cavern.

"No idea but isn't it odd that the last thing I remember was the crystals glowing crazily, filling the whole cavern with light. Now they're just normal looking white crystals. Don't know about you but my legs and calves are still killing me," he started to rub his trousered legs and was surprised when Robyn began to help him.

He didn't say anything but did begin to feel his muscles loosen up and he finally managed to straighten one leg out, although for a moment he thought his knee was going to break.

He let out a great sigh of relief then stretched the other leg out slowly, before realising he was effectively sitting astride Robyn. She looked slightly amused at how the two of them could look if someone had stumbled upon them at that very moment. He pulled up one leg and managed to put both to one side of Robyn who winced as she tried to move her own legs.

Scott saw her begin to massage her left leg, so he gently began to massage her rightone. She didn't complain but as he had found himself, it was initially painful as the circulation began to get working again.

Under different circumstances, the two of them rubbing each other's calves would have been quite sexy, but not now.

Robyn looked at him slyly in the torchlight.

"What happens in the cavern, stays in the cavern …"

He looked at her and grinned. "We're friends who at the moment only have each other, so we have to do what's needed. How's that feel now?"

She carefully stretched her right leg out and then held her knee as she winced with the pain.

Scott could only nod in sympathy. She managed to straighten it out and then moved her other leg until they sat roughly side by side with their legs pointing in opposite directions to each other, stretched out in front of them.

"That feels better. Not sure I want to stand up yet ,but at least they're beginning to feel more like normal," she said as she continued to massage her upper thigh whilst Scott did the same, only to his right ankle.

Robyn noted he started to look quite serious and in deep thought.

"What is it?" she asked gently.

"I, well, I, err…"

"Spit it out Scott please!"

"This sounds perhaps wrong but honestly, I'm sort of glad it's you with me down here."

Robyn didn't say anything but looked at him with a steady eye. He looked at her then down at his feet then back up and she nearly wanted to throttle him for beating about the bush.

"Well, Trina wouldn't cope like this. She'd probably be the worst person to be stuck with in an emergency, so heaven help Danny up on the surface as she's probably losing it. I'm sort of glad it's you…" he said and again looked away.

"Well, I'd prefer to be topside and not stuck down here at all. But, yes, I think I know what you mean. Danny may be great at the stress of city finance life on the stock exchange, but in reality he prefers an easy life and gets stressed out if anything goes wrong. A light bulb popping in our living room is too much for him! You on the other han …

Well, you are into adventure, discovery, exploration. That's why we get on so well and they both know that. So, we let them have their fun in the sun and we get to do the exploration.

Explorers are usually the sort of people who are good with unexpected situations so, yes, I'm glad it's you down here with me too."

She took him by surprise and kissed him on the lips then leaned away and put her hand up.

"That's for being level-headed and honest with me."

Scott smiled and said nothing. But something caught his eye, or rather he noticed he couldn't see as clearly. He looked down then chuckled as he picked up the wind-up torch and gave it several good turns of the handle making the light brighten back up.

"Thought it was me being dim!" he joked.

Robyn just shook her head then looked around the cavern. She spotted Scott's torch, just a metre or so away. She leaned over and rolled a little, grabbing it in the process and then shuffling back on to her backside.

She flicked the switch, but it was already in the on position and was as dead as her torch had been. "Well guess that confirms all the batteries are dead. Hey what about our smartphones?" Robyn wondered.

She fished inside her pocket and brought hers out as Scott did the same, but both screens were just as dead as the torches. Scott held the buttons to force restart his, but to no avail.

"This is getting eerie, these can last days on a full charge and mine was only down about five percent when we got to the cave entrance. Just how long have we been down here for it to die like that?"

Robyn shook her head, just as puzzled.

"Like you'd said, I'd have to guess at several days if it wasn't being used. If so, I'm surprised we've been unconscious for so long but equally, it would explain the layer of dust and why our eyes were gunged up. Let's try to stand."

They held each other by the arms and cautiously stood up with Scott almost collapsing as his legs didn't like the effort they were having to make. They finally stood up holding onto each other and stood, a little shakily, on their feet. Then Scott looked down and realised the wind up torch was on the floor to give them illumination.

"Bugger!"

Robyn didn't wait and stooped down, scooped up the torch then regained her footing whilst her legs screamed in agony at the unusual stress they were being put under.

She wobbled a little but with Scott's arms holding her she relaxed and gradually found she could stand on her own as he carefully let go.

"So, what do we do now then?" she asked

looking him in the eyes as the torchlight glinted off their eyeballs, giving both of them a scary horror appearance.

"Perhaps the gap to the upper cave has cleared? We ought to have a look don't you think?" he suggested, and she smiled.

"Just what I was thinking. Worth a shot. I'll go first with the torch," she didn't wait and set off up the slope wafting the torch back occasionally so Scott could see his way. She moved a little too fast, however.

"Oi! Speedy, slow down, I can't see where to put my feet, plus my bloody legs are killing me!"

"Sorry, here you go then slow coach. I'd have thought you would be the one faster than me seeing as you are the youngster!" she chuckled as he caught up with her and saw him scowl.

"Only by a year, nothing more."

They carried on, until the roof began to close in on them and it was plain there had been no change and the entrance to the first cave was blocked solid. Scott pushed past Robyn and banged hard on the biggest boulder.

"Hey, we're down here! We're alive!"

Silence.

He looked at her and shrugged. "It was worth a shot ..."

"We'll never dig that out. We're dead, I can tell you, we're dead." She burst into tears, catching Scott off guard as he knew Robyn was usually one tough cookie."

"Hey, hey, hey, now then." he embraced her, and she cried a little more before wiping the tears with her right hand.

"Sorry, but this was supposed to be an adventure. Seek out a cave locally and have a picnic, go back and regale everyone about how we discovered the cave paintings. But now …"

"And we will. Somehow. We'll be okay if we can keep it together until we find a way to the surface. If we can't get out this way then we will have to go back down to that crevice and see where that takes us. Yes?"

Robyn squeezed his hand and nodded, turned and together they began to head back down into the depths…

CHAPTER 6: DOWN DEEP INSIDE...

They stood at the metre wide ledge and peered over the edge.

"Looks deep and dark ..." Scott was having second thoughts as Robyn shone the torch beam into the depths and grimaced.

"Yes, but there, can you see? There is a steep set of the columns of basalt; if we get on to those we can edge along to our right where it narrows, step onto the columns on the other side and work our way back up."

She sat down on the ledge and slowly lowered herself onto one of the wider basalt columns.

Scott followed her lead then hesitated as Robyn reached a good section of the columns that almost made a continuous path. She looked up wondering what was keeping him.

"You OK?" she asked but with a growing concern.

"Erm, well, I'm ..." he stuttered, clearly embarrassed about something.

"You don't like heights?"

"Or depths for that matter. We've never had to do this sort of thing in our explorations before. Whilst there is a decent floor or path to walk on and a gentle slope then I'm OK. But I'm, I'm struggling to look down ..."

Robyn partially climbed back up and made sure

she had good footing then began to point out footholds.

"We've been good friends for a few years now, haven't we? So, trust me now. I'll go down first and don't look down.

Turn around so you are facing the rock wall. Get down onto your knees then slowly slide your body over the edge but don't come fully over. Slide your left foot down and I will guide it to a good safe spot. Then I'll guide your right foot to the other good spot. Trust me. OK?"

"OK."

Robyn nimbly lowered herself down and found a safe spot. Scott carefully adjusted his body position and did as she had suggested. Within just a couple of minutes, if that, he was stood next to Robyn who grinned at him.

"See, easy peasy!"

He smiled but still looked ill at ease with the darkness below them.

"Chin up! As I said, best not to look down. Now, I'll move ahead a few steps then shine the torch back, oh bugger ..." She fumbled with it as it was beginning to grow dim and she wound it back up bringing the light back to full intensity. "That's better, thought it was getting dimmer. So, I'll shine the torch back and point the beam to where you should step, you okay with that?"

"Haven't got much of a choice, have I? Yes, I trust you, carry on otherwise I might change my mind."

Over the next ten minutes they gradually made their way along one side of the crevasse then stepped over and came back along the other side. This time they ended up lower than Robyn had expected but she shone the torch ahead along the crevice back and forth then she spied something.

"There. Can you see it? Looks like another opening, could be another cave system so we'll head for it." Robyn said as she studied the view weighing up their options…and chances.

Scott could barely see what she had spotted but was content to follow her lead and so they slowly made their way along the basalt columns. Up, then down, then up a few feet then down as she used the columns as steppingstones.

They stopped to catch their breath and Robyn looked at the crevasse they were negotiating.

"I reckon this side and the other were joined sometime long ago then they split apart, perhaps from an earthquake as I can't think of anything else that could do it," she said without thinking about it.

"Trust you to analyse something like that even when our lives may well be in danger!" offered Scott as they started onwards, slowly managing to get a little higher and closer to the gap they'd spotted earlier.

Just when Scott thought they were almost there he suddenly saw something as Robyn swung the torch beam around and downwards deep into the crevice.

"Stop! Bring the beam back along the bottom, yes, stop. Oh my god ..."

They stared in shock at the body lying on a slightly wider section of the basalt columns about four or five metres down. Robyn looked carefully and worked out how she could get down to it.

"You stay here, I don't think there's much hope as there's quite a large dark stain on the ledge from the head. Must have some sort of full-length brown coverall on but I can't tell from here. I'll be careful, promise."

She didn't give Scott any time to say no, and he could only watch as she descended down towards the body aiming the torch beam to look out for a good route with plenty of footholds. It did leave him in darkness, so he leaned against the basalt column and took a deep breath.

It felt cold and hard to the touch, and he slid his hand along until he felt a rougher edge that he could hold on to and took another sigh, this time tinged with a little relief.

Robyn reached the body and wrinkled her nose. It had clearly been down there a very long time and was only partly decomposed. But what struck her was the recognition of something unique.

Firstly the 'coverall' was not one and secondly, it was clear to her the body was that of a Neanderthal or similar species. Waving the torch around she spotted what looked to be a thick stick or a branch which appeared burnt at one end, covered in soot and a thick layer of dust. Satisfied, she headed back up to Scott.

"Incredible! When we get out of here not only can we let the world know of the cave drawings, but it looks like we've also found a well-preserved corpse of a genuine caveman!"

"How do you know it's a he when he's got clothes on!"

"Put it like this, that's not an overall, it's a dense matt of dark brown hair coated in dust, and 'he' is naked even if his bits are a bit dried up! He must have been down there thousands of years and the dry conditions have preserved him well. There's also the remains of a roughly hewn wooden torch, so you never know, he may have been the one to do the drawings."

"That's all interesting I'm sure but there is one possibility to think about …" Scott observed.

"Eh?"

"He didn't seem to find a way out did he …"

"Oh. But then he's not us and perhaps he slipped and fell before he found a way to get out. Poor thing. Must have been terrified and slipped, falling to his death!"

They stood looking down at the body illuminated by the bleak torchlight for a few more minutes thinking about how the caveman's life had come to an abrupt end. Secretly each hoped they would not suffer the same fate.

Robyn wound up the torch again and aimed it forwards as they started along the columns, finally reaching the entrance to another cavern, the one they had spotted earlier. Scott noticed that Robyn seemed a little uncomfortable walking and feared she had hurt herself getting down to the body.

"You OK?" he asked as they ducked their heads and moved into the new cavern. Fortunately, it was a good height and they could both stand up and straighten their backs much to their relief. A few stalagmites were ahead along with corresponding stalactites hanging from the roof; Robyn went up to the largest stalagmite and leant against it. Scott noted it was about half her height.

"It's a bit embarrassing. I need a pee!" she looked down away from his face expecting a smart side crack.

"Oh, thank heavens for that. I thought you'd hurt yourself and wasn't going to tell me. To be honest, I need to go as well!"

They looked at each other and burst out laughing.

"Silly isn't it. We're adults yet something as basic as having a pee still causes us to clam up! Look I'll go the other side of that stalagmite over there and you do what you need to do the other side of yours. OK?" Robyn suggested and Scott nodded agreement.

She disappeared around the back of the stalagmite and as he undid his flies and began to pee he couldn't help laughing at the sounds they both made inside the cavern. It was like thunder! Especially with the torch light fading whilst they were both preoccupied and couldn't wind it up.

A funny thought struck him as he was almost finished.

"I wonder who'll play us when they make a movie about all this?" he called out and heard Robyn guffaw.

"George Clooney and Nicole Kidman?" she called back, and they both laughed. "You finished?" she added.

"Yes, thought you must have noticed as it's gone quiet now!"

"Cheeky bugger. When we get out of here I'll get Danny to tan your backside!" she said mockingly but smiled as she re-joined Scott, winding up the torch as she did so.

"Funny. Now where's the exit, this Algarve adventure is now wearing a bit thin," he retorted as Robyn cast the torchlight around then spotted a possible route.

She indicated the direction with the torch and they both headed off with her cautiously leading the way.

They had to duck their heads several times as the roof was very uneven, then the whole tunnel narrowed until it was impossible to carry on, even if they had tried crawling on their bellies.

Backing up, they retraced their steps back to the wider cavern with the stalagmites and stalactites. Robyn was a bit despondent by now.

"It must have been a vein of soft rock that was eroded away. There has to be another way.

Otherwise, otherwise …" her voice trailed off to a whisper.

"Don't go down that road. There is another way, but we just need to take a moment, rest up and then have another look around."

Robyn sighed then turned the torch off to save the battery, much to Scott's amusement considering it was the wind up one and the others didn't work. It was almost pitch black which made Scott uncomfortable, but he still instinctively looked around then moved his head back and forth. Robyn could tell from the subtle sounds he was up to something, but was puzzled. She turned on the torch.

"Robyn, turn it off."

"Eh? Thought you hated the dark?"

"Turn it off, please."

She did so but was puzzled at this sudden change in her friend. She could just see that he was slowly looking around and became perplexed.

"What's up? I can see you are searching for something."

"Ahh, that's just it. You *shouldn't* be able to see me at all should you? Can you also feel something?"

Robyn started to look around then realised what he meant.

"Wow. There's a slight breeze. It's also slightly lighter over in that direction," she ventured.

Scott took the torch off her and turned it on, slowly picking his way across the cavern floor to a new gap in the rock face as for once, Robyn was left to follow him as he entered it. They seemed to walk for several minutes but it could have been an hour, before Scott let out a gasp. He found what appeared to be a rockfall sloping upwards, a scree slope; indeed, he gasped in delight.

There was a tiny sliver of daylight visible higher up at the top of the slope.

Eagerly they started to scramble up, but quickly stopped as rocks and rubble slid down taking then back a few metres. They slowed their pace and steadily picked their way back up the slope until they reached the daylight crack. Clawing away at the rubble they widened the hole, almost dazzled by the sunlight. After just a few short minutes Robyn pushed up through the hole quickly followed by Scott.

They had escaped from the dark depths.

CHAPTER 7: SHOCK…

Utterly alien.

That was the view that confronted them as they shielded their eyes from the bright sunshine.

"Where's …" started Robyn as she looked on with shock and horror.

"The vegetation?" Scott muttered as he surveyed the barren rocky landscape that should have been the valley they had looked down upon when they had stood at the original entrance to the caverns.

There was not a trace of any form of greenery, no vegetation of any sort, size or shape. No field system or signs of life. The valley looked as if it had been sandblasted. The stream at the bottom still dribbled along, but had none of the usual wetland vegetation you would associate with a water course.

As they looked on in horror it struck them, the lemon and orange groves, all the trees were gone with only small, barely discernible burnt-out stumps left dotting the landscape, indeed there was no tree cover left whatsoever.

Scott looked and pointed off to their left, down the valley. Robyn gasped.

The motorway bridge as it crossed the valley was virtually gone, a few hints of a couple of the original concrete and metal pylons that had carried it over the valley remained, whilst the rubble had blocked the valley. What little water still flowing had managed to find a way by eroding the hillside and bypassing the remains. Robyn began to shake her head in disbelief.

"They, they finally did it. The idiots finally did it. There must have been a nuclear war and the fallout has destroyed all life on the surface." She sat down heavily and couldn't find any more words to adequately cover her growing despair.

Scott looked about at the landscape then up and around the sky.

"Surely someone will have survived?" he muttered, not really expecting an answer as he shielded his eyes from the bright sunlight whilst trying to spot aircraft contrails.

Robyn held her head in her hands and was shaking it negatively. Wanting to cry, she couldn't say anything as she thought about friends and family, her elderly mother back in Wales, her sister and her family in Bristol. If the Algarve was like this, then what hope for the rest of Europe and the UK? The world?

Scott stood next to her as a thought struck him.

"I tell you what. We'd best try to get up to the original cave entrance and see if there is any sign of what happened to Trina and Danny."

He held out his hand, Robyn took it and he hauled her to her feet. She nodded and looked up the side of the valley where she thought the entrance should be. She pointed and Scott followed her line of sight, agreed on the direction and they set off, carefully picking their way slowly up the hillside.

It took them roughly what seemed like half an hour, but without their smart phones working they had no real sense of the time passing. Finally, Scott shouted as he had pulled ahead by a few metres.

"This looks like the path that we thought would come down this side of the valley."

He started to walk up it and was quickly joined by Robyn, who at least felt a bit better now there was a proper path.

She bumped into Scott without warning as she had her head down and was in deep thought. He grunted and she was about to say something when he gently guided her round to stand next to him.

Two heavily weatherworn and effectively bleached human skeletons lay sprawled across the path, both looking like they were heading down slope. Some of the bones were mixed up and scattered and indeed some were missing. Robyn thought she was going to faint but took a deep breath and just about held it together.

Scott looked at what remained of the skeletons clothing and indeed two of what could have been rucksacks, but like the bodies, there was not much left to help identify them. As soon as he touched what seemed like the remains of a shirt, the fabric disintegrated to dust. He looked again at the skeletons as he felt a surge of emotion engulf him at the loss of their partners.

"They must have tried to get down to the valley floor and get help. Oh Katrina …" he couldn't help but cry at her fate and Robyn held him and joined in his tears as she thought of Danny and what it must have been like for them both as they perished.

Several minutes passed while they had their heads down as they gave silent prayers for their partners, then Robyn noticed the light level seemed to be getting darker. She looked up and shook her head.

"Looks like a storm brewing. Wonder if we should head back down to the cave entrance we came from?"

Scott shrugged then looked up the slope. "We're probably closer to the original entrance so let's head that way. Not sure about you but I'm so caked in dust that I don't mind getting wet, it would feel good, like a shower and might do us some good."

"OK, let's go."

As the first raindrop hit clothing, it didn't register.

The next large droplet splattered on Scott's arm and he grabbed it in pain.

"What the …"

Lightning flashed above the hillside from the darkening clouds and another droplet struck Robyn on the cheek and she winced.

"Bloody hell! This is strong acid rain! Quick! We need to get under cover from this before it belts it down."

Together they scrambled up the rough, and at times faint, path until suddenly they came across the place where it seemed, not long earlier, they had all been enjoying the sun and a bit of banter. They barely noticed the remains of the two-fold up chairs Danny had brought along. The acid rain started to fall harder; they dived into the cave entrance then crept further into it and looked back out, watching the deluge from apparent safety.

The hiss of the rain on the ground became deafening and seemed to go on for hours as the sky gradually got darker. Then they realised the sun had to be setting.

"Didn't think I'd be pleased about being back inside the cave. Did you?" Scott said, thinking out loud as he wound up the torch and turned it on, briefly dazzling them in the process.

He pushed it into the cave floor for stability, so it cast a light to illuminate them better.

"No, but we should be safe here until it passes over and let's face it, no point in trying to go anywhere whilst it is night outside." She looked downhearted, indeed heartbroken and Scott gently put his arm around her waist but said nothing and she snuggled in a little, in appreciation of the gesture.

"Yeah, I guess we also now know why no one came to look for us if all hell was breaking loose out there. I guess we ought to try to get some sleep, but I could do with some water."

He rummaged in his rucksack and brought out his bottle which was only one third full since he'd used some of it to try to clear their eyes and mouths when they were deep down in the cave earlier.

"Best not go mad using it up, probably better to just take a sip. If the stream is being fed by this rain then it's likely we can't drink from it. Our bottles may be the only water we have," pointed out Robyn as the torchlight gently illuminated her face.

"Good point indeed." He took a sip then handed it to her and she took a small sip too before taking the cap from him and screwing it tightly on, so as to not risk losing any of the precious, possibly lifesaving, liquid.

She pulled her rucksack around and positioned it carefully before lowering her head on to it. Scott smiled ruefully and did the same and they lay together, cuddled up with no further words said between them.

They were lost in their own thoughts as questions on why and how everything had happened and why they had somehow survived, swirled inside their respective heads as they dropped off to sleep. It came despite the bright lightning flashes and accompanying thunderous roar outside as the storm raged on through the night.

\#

It was a good thing the torch didn't require batteries as they had not turned it off before going to sleep, but it was the light flooding into the cave from outside that awoke them.

Robyn looked around a little sleepily then at Scott as he shook his head and pushed his fringe out of his eyes.

"We didn't dream it then?" she asked, not really wanting to hear his answer. Scott just shook his head and stood up as he flexed his muscles to get rid of any cramp he felt with sleeping on the rough floor of the cavern. Robyn did the same, then they both poked their heads cautiously out of the cave entrance.

It just seemed like a typical Algarvian morning with lovely bright sunshine and a slight but pleasant breeze. Then reality struck home at the sheer desolate nature of the valley and landscape before them, reds, browns and yellows, assaulted their eyes.

Crawling out, Robyn spotted something badly rusted and went over to look, picking up a metal rod with just a bit of fabric still clinging to it.

The fold up chairs Danny had brought out expecting to use them for himself and Katrina to sunbathe whilst the 'adventurous duo', as Danny sometimes called Scott and Robyn, went off exploring the cave.

She felt cold inside as Scott took it from her, examined it then kicked at the loose soil exposing some more of the chairs. There was no doubt, both were still set up as Robyn remembered when she'd come back to the entrance to tell Danny and Trina they were going to explore deeper. The remains however looked odd, so corroded and worn down, that it seemed difficult to think they had been there just a few days.

More like years.

Centuries...

"If only they'd been more adventurous like us ..." she said quietly. Scott was close enough to hear her and nodded slowly.

"Simply wasn't in their nature. High pressure jobs in the city, so for them going on holiday was a chance to simply unwind and do nothing. They often say that likeminded souls don't gel and that opposites attract so I fell for Katrina, you for Danny. Just one of those things I guess."

"Yeah, just one of those things ..." Robyn said as her voice trailed away to nothing. She bent her head and muttered a short prayer for their deceased other halves and Scott lowered his head too as a mark of respect.

A few minutes of silence then Robyn lifted her head up and seemed a little different, more like her normal self. "Don't know about you but I'm getting hungry and I'm parched. We don't have much in the way of supplies so we'd best stay inside the cave entrance for shade and check out what we have.

If everything is destroyed and there's no food out there then we're stuffed."

Scott nodded and they headed back into the cave, picked up their rucksacks and began to empty them out.

Both: sunscreen; still needed.

Robyn: Emergency kit with band aids and some skin healing cream; still useful and the cream had not deteriorated, surprisingly.

Scott: one litre sized bottle with less than a third of his water left but a smaller half litre bottle of orange squash nearly full and diluted ready to drink, incredibly drinkable as he took a sip to check and put the thumbs up.

Robyn: one almost full litre sized bottle of water and also a half bottle of orange squash, hopefully ready to drink.

They looked at her bottle and she shook it up then opened it and took a small sip. Just like Scott's, it was still okay, much to their relief.

Robyn: a large sized plastic tub with sandwiches in, originally for her and Danny. Four sandwiches of sardines, her favourite and four of ham and cheese for Danny. They smelled just as fresh as when she'd made them. Odd…

Scott: no sandwiches as Katrina had those in her rucksack. Robyn looked at him and had to smile.

"Looks like you'll have to starve then," she said cheekily as Scott made a sour face at her and she relented. "OK, you can have the ham and cheese ones then if you are good."

Scott wasn't quite sure what sort of being good would qualify but he was pleased she was so organised. Anyway, he wasn't keen on sardines so that was a blessing in disguise.

Both rucksacks still had their sunhats, bought locally and made of cloth so at least they would have some shade for their heads. Otherwise, there was just a few chocolate bars and a couple of slices of a Madeira cake that their hostess, Judith, had made for them during their stay. It too seemed as fresh as if it had just been made.

Judith…

Without realising it both turned their thoughts briefly to what may have happened to her. Scott broke the short silence.

"Well, we can make this last for a day at least?"

Robyn looked at Scott stunned.

"Seriously? We might have to make this small lot last days, maybe even three or four at the very least. We can't eat it all up until we have found somewhere with food and, let's face it, if it was a nuclear war then we might not be able to eat anything."

"We could starve …" muttered Scott solemnly and Robyn stood up and looked at him closely.

"Hey, we'll find something. But we just have to be careful at the moment until we do."

"I know, but I'm getting hungry. As far as I can remember the last meal was the continental breakfast before we set off for our walk and God knows when that was."

Scott searched his rucksack and brought out his 'back up shirt' as he liked to call it, and his shorts from, well it seemed like another time entirely.

"Why ...?" Robyn began to ask looking at the shirt.

"I always have a spare shirt. From my boy scout's days. Always carry spare clothes. Mind you over the years it's ended up being a long-sleeved shirt in case the weather changed when on holiday.

Robyn just shook her head but was secretly impressed at some of his 'forward' planning.

They packed everything carefully back into the rucksacks then stepped outside. Robyn surveyed the view before them. She looked into the distance, out to sea.

Or at least she should have been able to see the coastline. Portimao's tallest buildings should have been visible as she remembered seeing them from their holiday villa balcony, yet they were absent. Off to the right they could see the coastline stretching away around to Lagos, but it was hard to make out any buildings, indeed any sign of the coastal town.

In fact, they should have been able to see the coastline. Yet, it seemed to be another couple of kilometres further out. As if the sea, or rather the Atlantic Ocean had receded.

They stood and gawped at the odd view.

"This couldn't happen in just a couple of days. Could it?" asked Scott, thinking out loud.

"No," whispered Robyn as she took in the view with its implications. "I don't really know what to say or think. I did climatology as part of my geology and geography PhD and it was all about global temperature and CO^2 rising leading to sea levels rising, not falling. That was the all-out danger that the politicians kept ignoring.

Not sea level dropping. It doesn't feel any warmer than when we set off from the villa the other day and I don't think even nuclear war could do this. I'm stumped."

"Makes two of us then. Perhaps we'd best head off and see if we can find any remaining houses or villas and look for signs of life and food?" Scott looked at her and could see she was thinking the same. Robyn nodded and started off back down the rough, and in places, barely visible track.

"For now, let's see if we can get to the motorway and follow the road system into Portimao and hope that something survived like a shop or supermarket," she said.

Scott had a thought. "Or someone's home..?"

"Guess so, if it comes to it. I have a feeling there won't be many survivors, if any…"

On that point they both fell silent as they made their way along the rough track.

CHAPTER 8: DESOLATION

Bleak.

As they steadily made their way down from the cave, Robyn kept a wary eye out in case another storm brewed up quickly. She noted Scott too was keeping a watchful eye on the sky as he glanced around but figured that, like herself, he was probably just hoping to spot another living being.

A sign they were not the only ones...

Or for that matter anything alive would have given her some hope. She realised something that should have been obvious.

"There's no insect life."

"Say what?" asked Scott as he managed to avoid a small rock but nearly skidded on some loose stones and scree and cursed somewhat loudly.

"There's no insect life. None. We're normally having to bat away mozzies, wasps, you name it, all manner of insects that usually annoy us. But there's nothing."

She bent over and pulled a rock up. "See? Normally there's loads of insects and worms and the like under a rock as it protects them from the harsh ultraviolet rays of the sun. But still nothing, not a single thing.

It's, it's like the surface of Mars..." Robyn shook her head, worried at the implications.

"Even under what I'd have thought the worst-case conditions, insects technically dominate our planet and get everywhere. There is nothing I can think of that can wipe even them out. Insects are one of the most resilient forms of life on earth."

"Robyn, seriously, you're beginning to freak me out even more now."

"Sorry, but if the insect population has crashed most vegetation and cultivation needs them for pollination, so if they're gone ..."

"Most higher land based life either feeds on them or on the plants that they need to survive. Did Danny ever tell you that you're a really cheerful person?"

She slapped him on the arm but only lightly as the mention of her husband's name briefly brought happy memories back. Scott looked at her as he too found his thoughts turning back to Katrina.

"It must have been quick for them. Odd though that there didn't seem to be any bones broken. You'd have thought if there was a blast wave then they'd been bowled over and so broken something." Scott mused out loud. Robyn thought about this then nodded in agreement.

"If it was nuclear then perhaps it was the radiation overwhelming them on the spot. But..."

"But?"

"Their remains weren't damaged but eroded. By time. I mean, a *long time ...*"

"Stop it Robyn, it's bad enough as it is without us going to the extreme with our theories. Let's keep going shall we and see what we come across."

She nodded silently and together the continued for an hour before reaching the valley floor where a small stream trickled along. Scott lowered himself to his haunches and gently dipped his little fingertip into the small flow of water. He pulled it out sharp-ish as Robyn gasped then he burst out laughing.

She was not amused.

"You daft bugger. I thought it was acidic and had burnt you!"

He shrugged and slowly put his hand into the water then cupped it and brought up a small handful of the liquid to his face and sniffed.

"Doesn't seem to have any smell, or rather it seems like I remember a freshwater stream should be like." Before she could say stop, he sipped at the water in his hand then seemed to move his head slightly as he allowed his taste buds to check it out.

He swallowed and smiled.

"Seems legit! Doesn't have any nasty aftertaste but actually is almost tasteless."

Robyn sat on the side of the bank of the stream and fished in Scott's rucksack. She brought out his bottle of water then rummaged in her own rucksack and brought out hers. Deftly she tipped his remaining water into her bottle completely filling it up then put the remaining small amount into her orange squash bottle. She handed his now empty litre bottle back to him.

"There you go then. Fill it up. If we keep it

separate for now, so we know we have one with our original water and drink from that, then use the other when we have no choice. Here..." she quickly picked up a sharp looking small rock and scratched a mark on the plastic cap. "There, we'll know which is which now."

"Beauty and brains, that's why I love you ..." he replied then looked at her hastily. "I mean, err, you know, it's why we get on so well as friends."

"Good recovery Scott, good recovery." Robyn looked at him wryly. "The sentiment is appreciated under the circumstances. Now, if we head off in a diagonal line up the other side of this valley in the direction of Portimao, at some point we'll come across the motorway or what remains of it, plus we must surely encounter a villa or house along the way."

Scott was relieved and stood, holding out his hand, but being independent Robyn just smiled and stood of her own accord. They looked about then struck off following a faint trail heading in a line that looked like it would have to encounter the remains of the motorway and by following that, they'd surely come across some form of habitation.

The sun climbed higher; it was a hot cloudless day, a mixed blessing, mused Robyn considering how quickly the storm had almost caught them out the evening before. She spotted where the original motorway bridge had reached their side of the valley and could see that enough was left overhanging to give some shelter if needed.

It reassured her knowing they wouldn't be caught out in the open if an acid rainstorm did develop and they hadn't strayed too far from it.

Scott stopped, wiped his brow and shook his head. "I so want to take my shirt and trousers off."

"Well, I'm scorched in this but we need to get sunscreen on if we do take them off. Plus do our arms and legs otherwise we might regret it later."

Scott looked across and pointed. "Perhaps best to get under the overhang of the motorway so we're in the shade?"

"Good idea."

They struck off towards the nearest part of the remains and before long clambered their way down and under the overhanging remains of the motorway. Scott immediately stripped off his shirt and stood panting in the shade. He opened his rucksack and after a brief search triumphantly brought out his tube of sunscreen. Spreading it over his chest and shoulders and reaching as far as he could around his back he wasn't taking notice of anything else until Robyn sidled up to him, put some of the cream on her right hand and hinted he should turn round.

She massaged it into his back to grateful sounds from Scott then stepped back, trying to ignore his physique.

"That better?" she asked innocently, and he grinned as he nodded happily.

Robyn then peeled off her blouse and squirted

some of the cream onto her hand, knowing Scott was trying not to watch.

"We're grown-ups you know. I have got my bra on, silly! I'll do my front if you don't mind but, well, can you do my back for me?" she asked.

"Well, you helped me, so one good turn, eh?"

Scott sat for a few moments as Robyn carefully applied the cream to her exposed skin then handed the tube back to Scott and turned round. He gently massaged the cream into her back but stopped at her bra strap.

"What's up, don't stop!"

"But ..." Scott hesitated.

"Don't by coy Scott, lift it up and get some cream under it, nothing to be ashamed about. Besides ...It's not like our other halves will now be bothered, will they?"

Scott knew she had a point so carried on until her back was done down to her shorts.

They both tied their tops about their midriff and, turning their backs to each other, changed from the trousers into their shorts. They set off back up the hill until they reached the remains of the motorway.

It was stark and horrific all at once. Brown and red patches of what was probably rust along with a wide variety of darker 'sludges' indicated where cars and other vehicles had come to a terrible end. A few long sections suggested lorries with some metal and plastic just about identifiable.

Occasionally skeletal remains could be seen in

amongst them and as they passed them the two companions shook their heads in abject sorrow.

"Just how long could this have taken. It beggars belief that it's just been a few days." Scott said out loud as he tried to grasp the reality of the events that must have taken place.

"Seriously, it's freaking me out. I'm not an expert on materials but, this looks like hundreds, maybe thousands of years. How can that be? For that matter, if that's the case…how come we survived all that time?" Robyn looked around in sadness and utter disbelief.

They carried on and began to recognise where they were. They approached what appeared to be a junction where the road was elevated above the surrounding terrain. Stumps indicated motorway signage had collapsed and eroded almost to nothing, not showing a turn off to a village or indeed off to Portimao, but that it was the right direction.

As they approached it they realised the joining road led down past a village they had not bothered to look up when they first arrived on holiday but at least there was a chance to find buildings and perhaps even anything resembling shops or perhaps amenities.

They turned down the road and looked on in despair at the ruined buildings scattered across the landscape. Not one was fully intact with most having caved in roofs, collapsed walls and not a single window left intact.

"There must have been more earthquakes after we passed out. It's like one of those apocalyptic movies I used to like watching. Now it's insanely real," Robyn said as they continued down the gentle slope of the road, passing collapsed buildings as they did so.

They had to sidestep past several sections of roadway that had crumpled under extreme heat at some point and there were potholes everywhere. They stopped outside a villa that seemed in slightly better condition with a fancy driveway leading up to it.

Scott looked at her and she nodded, knowing what he was thinking.

The door was smashed, not boding very well for them as they pushed past it.

"Hello? Anyone here?" Robyn's voice seemed to echo through the remains of the building, but they were only met with silence. They slowly made their way into what seemed to be the main lounge to be confronted by six skeletal remains. It was difficult for them to work out at first what gender each had been.

They were all coated in a thick layer of dust where the acid rain had apparently turned in to a solid mass. It crumbled to dust as Scott gently touched the nearest body and several of the bones also disintegrated.

Robyn called out as she had moved back into the hallway, then found the kitchen.

"Scott, **Scott**?"

Scott heard a large crashing sound and rushed to find her. Robyn stood next to what should have been a refrigerator, but the remains of the door were scattered on the floor. Piles of dust was all that remained on the fridge shelves, those that somehow were only just intact.

"I barely touched the door as I tried to open it and it just came off in my hand. I didn't really expect to find anything edible, but this is just awful."

Scott walked over to a set of wall units and gingerly tried to open one. The hinges held but the handle disintegrated as he pulled, but his eyes widened at seeing a variety of tinned products. The labels were just dust, but he went to pick one up.

It broke up in his hands and the contents, whatever they had been, were damp but acrid and smelled revolting.

Robyn joined him and picked up a larger can and the same thing happened. They tried every tin but to no avail.

"It's like they've been cooked without being opened then they've gone off." she mused and shook her head as they wandered back into the lounge, not wanting to face seeing the bodies, then headed back out into the hallway and both eyed up the stairs.

The steps were made of stone and so Scott put one foot on the first step, tested his weight then slowly made his way up, followed by Robyn. They felt the upper landing floor move slightly then suddenly collapse just as Scott stepped onto it with one foot and together they quickly backed off onto the stone stairs.

"Not sure about you but I don't trust it, do you?" Scott looked at Robyn and she shook her head so they turned back and went downstairs to the kitchen again.

Robyn had a thought and even though she knew what to expect, she went over to the sink and turned the taps on.

Nothing, not a drop issued from it and indeed the tap handle came off in her hand.

She sat on the floor lost for words and Scott joined her.

They sat quietly for several minutes, neither wanting to voice what each was probably thinking but eventually Robyn gave out a large sigh.

"If this is typical of everywhere else, then we're really well and truly screwed!"

"Can't think it will be different anywhere else," Scott replied dourly and was about to say something else about starving to death when he cocked his head to one side, listening.

"What?" Robyn asked, worried.

"Listen." They did so then she too heard it.

Thunder in the distance.

They quickly ran outside and looked at the large dark storm clouds gathering, and several violent flashes seemed to strike the higher ground, not far from where they had set off from the cave.

"We'll never get back to the cave in time." Scott needn't have said anything as it was pretty obvious, but Robyn pulled him back into the remains of the villa.

As they did so they heard the sharp hiss of the acid rain strike the outside grounds followed by hailstones that had to be almost fist sized. They heard the roof being pummelled by them.

They quickly checked the rooms, most had some part of the ceiling fallen in and part of the roof with gaping holes and they could see the storm clouds and lightning as the rain began to fall harder, splattering on the floor where it got through the holes in ceiling and roof.

One room, quite small and probably a storage room seemed intact; they opened the door thankful it did not fall apart, crammed inside and pulled the door shut.

The storm intensified and in the darkness with bright flashes illuminating their feet from the gap under the door they sat huddled together, terrified it wasn't going to be enough protection.

They could now hear the gale force winds adding their destructive force to the acid rain and huge hailstones and could imagine now how the buildings had become so battered, if indeed it had been thousands of years that had elapsed.

Perhaps this was now their time, perhaps their fate was catching up with them …

CHAPTER 9: THE WANDERERS

On into the night and still the storm raged. Scott felt Robyn trembling and, knowing their heads were close together, he gently whispered to her.

"You doing okay Robyn?"

"No. Always hated thunder and lightning and struggled a bit with it when we were in the cave. But knowing there's nowhere to go to, it feels all the more horrible. Plus, I'm getting cold. Help me get my blouse back on."

"Glad you mentioned that as I didn't want to disturb you but I'm pretty cold too. It started off quite muggy but now it's night the temperature must have fallen. We don't even know now what season it really is, do we!"

She just muttered something, and they sat up, unwrapped their tops from their waists and put them back on. Without thinking, they snuggled up together to keep warm.

It continued to rain heavily with wave after wave of thunder and lightning passing over but somehow, despite it, they managed to fall asleep.

Dawn broke and the storm was weakening as Robyn opened her eyes. She felt Scott was slumped against her, still fast asleep. She carefully brushed his hair up away from his eyes and he stirred but didn't wake.

She knew she'd always had some feelings for

him and had always looked forward to the holidays she and Danny shared with Scott and Katrina.

Despite the age old saying that opposites attract, she knew that sometimes it was like minded people with shared interests that could work well as a couple in many cases.

She loved Danny but, she also loved the way Scott brought out the explorer in her. Their adventures exploring the countryside instead of the beach made her feel alive for those, often much too short, two-week holidays once a year as a foursome.

Scott opened his eyes and yawned, rolled over a little but realising the 'accommodation' was a little cramped, rolled back only to look straight into Robyn's eyes.

"You comfy m'lord?" she asked, then broke out into a smile. "Thanks for last night. I had a weak moment or two, but glad you are here with me."

"Don't mention it. You're stuck with me anyway so hope my snoring didn't keep you awake?" he joked as she lightly thumped him on his arm.

"Nit! What with that thunder last night, I wouldn't have known," she lied and quickly changed tack. "Let's stick our heads outside and see what it's like now." She pushed gently at Scott, and he moved so she could stand and together they pushed the door of the closet open, cautiously stepping out trying to clear the cramp in their legs.

Apart from a few pools of water that didn't

look inviting, the sun had already dried up the outside with little sign there had been a storm apart from what seemed like a receding cloud bank on the distant horizon, out to what should have been the Atlantic Ocean.

Except for a few, somewhat too close for comfort, black marks nearby showing lightning strikes. They wandered out, slinging the rucksacks on their backs and examined the scorch marks.

"Phew, a bit close for comfort I'd say." Scott muttered as they headed down the road. "Really glad we have the sun hats and sunglasses. This barren desolate scenery is pretty harsh under this sun."

Noticing Robyn wasn't saying anything, he turned and walked backwards as he looked at her quizzically.

"Turn around you daft thing. There's no hospitals or doctors now so we can't have an accident!" she said but he still kept looking at her before turning round so he didn't fall over.

"You OK?" he asked.

"OK, if you must know, I'm in a bit of pain. Not anything nasty but, don't laugh, I need a crap!"

Scott mouthed 'Ooh' as he looked back at her, but oddly he wasn't disturbed by her confession.

"You're not alone, so do I, but I've managed to hold on so far."

"But what do we do? There's no running water, most of the toilets are on the second floor that we've seen so far, so they're probably unusable.

Plus, there's no toilet paper!"

"I didn't pack anything into the rucksacks as a backup because we didn't expect to be away from our villa for so long." Scott shrugged as he tried to look apologetic.

"It's alright, how could we ever have know what was about to happen?"

Scott had got his binoculars out and was scanning the landscape then stopped suddenly, fixated on one spot. He pointed off to their left, back up into the low hills.

"I can see a one story villa up there so a toilet would be on the ground floor. Not sure if there is a road that takes us there from here but we could just head off in a straight line.

No one's going to complain as we clamber across people's properties now are they!"

"How far do you think it is?" she asked.

"A kilometre, at worst, two?"

"OK, I'll hold, I'll have to!"

Scott struck off at the next bend on the left and they steadily made their way ever closer to the villa. They passed a house and Scott dashed in to see if it would save them the journey but came out shaking his head.

"Upstairs by my reckoning plus the stairs have collapsed so can't get up there anyway." he said, dismayed.

They carried on but it was another half hour before they finally reached a driveway that led up to the villa.

Approaching cautiously, they found the front door locked but pitted and deformed, probably from the acid rainfall; Scott pushed against it only for it to disintegrate.

It was clearly a well to do place but like everywhere else, as soon as they touched anything it disintegrated, crumbled and turned to dust. Only the walls seemed to be solid, explaining why so far all the properties they'd found were still standing, just! For how long that would be the case was another matter entirely.

Scott wandered into a large kitchen area when he heard a yelp from Robyn, and he rushed back and looked around for her.

He heard her again and followed a short corridor almost bumping into her stood looking in horror.

It was a bathroom with toilet, but Robyn had cried out because there were skeletal remains scattered around the toilet bowl.

"Oh, what a way to go, having a crap!" Scott couldn't help himself saying at the bizarre sight.

"I, I, can't do it, not having seen that." Robyn stared aghast at the sight and thought of the person's last moments having taken place on the toilet.

"Well statistically, I guess it would have to have happened to someone. Look, there may not be running water, but I'll get rid of the remains. Just give me a moment, OK?"

She nodded but walked out back down the

corridor and found the lounge. The windows no longer existed but she took her mind off the bathroom scene with the view she imagined the original occupants would have enjoyed, heaven knows how many years ago that was.

After a few minutes Scott entered.

"Your bathroom awaits m'lady. Err, this may seem odd, well, so far everything has been odd, but …" he brought his hand from behind his back and presented her with some material that she vaguely recognised.

"That's your spare shirt you always carry with you. I can't use that."

"I thought you'd say that but too late, I've torn it into strips for you to use for, well, you know this and er, well, you know, the other that ladies have to put up with …"

For some reason, Robyn felt all emotional as she knew that if it was Danny standing there, he'd never sacrifice his shirt for anything. She knew at that instant; Scott would do anything for her …

She walked up to him, kissed him on the lips whilst taking hold of the material and headed back to the bathroom.

Scott headed outside for he too had to go, and he didn't care if it was going to be outside as he held on to a few of the strips remaining of his other shirt. Who was around to see him - no one!

#

"Scott? Scott? Where are you love?"

Robyn walked out the front entrance of the villa, relieved at last but concerned that she couldn't see or hear Scott.

"SCOTT?"

"Hey, give a guy a bit of privacy, won't you?" she heard his voice and quickly walked over to a garden shed then stepped back and turned her back on him.

He finished off and wiped then clambered out of what remained of the shed.

"I told you I also needed to go. Anyway, no harm done. You OK now?"

"You could have said you were going to find somewhere."

"You were in a bit of a hurry yourself, remember? Come on, best find a stream eh?"

"Too right! I'm not holding hands with you until we've both washed!"

They suddenly burst out laughing and sat on the ground.

"You couldn't write this stuff even if you tried!" Robyn said and looked at Scott who just grinned.

"Well, before I ahh, did my stuff, I spotted something interesting further down the valley. If we'd kept on our original road we'd have come to that supermarket we used a few days into our holiday, the one Judith had recommended."

"So, if we just double back a couple of kilometres or so to that small stream and wash, then head over there?" she suggested, and Scott smiled.

"See, we're on the same page after all. Let's go. Lead on M'c Duff!"

CHAPTER 10: OF TINS AND A SLEEP

Although it took almost half an hour, as they couldn't remember exactly where they'd spotted the stream, once washed and dried in the sun they headed back and after almost two hours they had finally reached the remains of the supermarket.

That was a generous description considering most of it had collapsed in on itself.

"Guess they never thought to build it to last hundreds or maybe even thousands of years." Robyn mused as they clambered as carefully as they could over some of the fallen down outer walls.

"It really does feel like it has gotta been several centuries. It's not looking hopeful is it ..." Scott looked about and just as they'd found in the villas and houses, as they touched items, in most cases they turned to dust or at least crumbled into chunks. In many cases it was hard to even work out what they had originally been in the first place.

Shelving had collapsed throughout what they could see of the building but on one side there appeared to be lots of tinned items and they headed over as safely as they could.

Excitement grew as many tins appeared intact but just as Scott eagerly picked up one of them, Robyn stopped him.

"The can's bulging out. Means that the

contents have gone off. I think it's something to do with botulism or something like that. I think I read that some cans have been found to be OK after about a hundred years, you know, in shipwrecks and the like, but I have a horrible feeling we somehow 'slept' for longer than that."

Scott looked about and his face soured.

"They're all like it." He went to sit down on them, dejected, but Robyn stopped him.

"No, if they're bulging then the seals may be on the verge of breaking so best not to chance it and get a cut bum! I can assure you I'm not examining that part of you unless absolutely necessary and in really *dire* medical need!"

They checked out a few more rows but everything was the same when it came to the tins. Deflated, they headed back outside and sat on the remains of the parking lot brick wall.

Robyn handed Scott a small chunk of a sandwich from her rucksack, and he took it and examined it for a moment.

"How much have we got left?"

"Just a couple of sandwiches left, a bit of the Madeira cake and apart from that bottle of water we filled with stream water, half a bottle of orange squash and a small amount of our original water in the other bottle," she replied solemnly.

"I'm starving now …"

"I know love, but, I don't have anything to say to make it better."

Scott popped the small chunk of the sandwich

into his mouth and slowly, ever so slowly, chewed on it, trying to make it last. The ham and cheese tantalised his taste buds; they almost cred out to know why they couldn't sample more juicy morsels.

He swallowed and took a sip from the original water bottle. This was the one with the water they had originally brought with them before the calamity, and he saw there was just a small amount left. He ceremoniously handed it to Robyn who nodded and drank the final drops of the precious liquid after making her small portion of a sardine sandwich last as long as she could.

She also wryly noticed that there was a hint the sardines were going off which was not surprising considering the hot weather.

"Well, that's that. We've no choice now but to start on the other bottle. If we take it steady then we can either head back to that small stream, before another acid storm hits us, to keep filled up or press on down to the coast and see what we can find," she noted.

"OK, so let's press on to the coast and you never know, we may even find a working toilet on the way!" Scott suggested and laughed half-heartedly.

Robyn giggled. "You daft bat. Well, it won't be for a number two I can tell you as we've hardly eaten anything over the last few days so there won't be 'owt to come out', so to speak."

"Well let's make sure if we have a pee, we don't accidentally contaminate our drinking supply eh?"

"That's a really good point. Oh well, sun's well past midday by my reckoning, best start now and perhaps find somewhere with some shelter in case there is a storm. We don't want to be caught out in one like we almost were last night." Robyn had her thinking head on now and Scott admired her spirit.

"Lead on then boss."

"Glad you recognise my superiority, mister!"

They looked at each other and had to smile despite the situation. They set off down the slight slope of the road in the direction of the coast and the outskirts of Portimao. As they got closer to the more densely urbanised districts it was obvious it was likely to be dangerous.

Buildings had collapsed, roads were blocked with what must have been crashed vehicles of all sizes plus the building debris.

They changed tack and skirted to the side of the town where the roads appeared to be less cluttered and with fewer buildings. Less potential danger.

The sun was getting lower however, so Robyn indicated to a villa that seemed to be in better shape than most and they pushed the entrance gates open, which became unhinged from the wall as they did so and fell heavily, making a huge noise that reverberated around the area.

"Well, if there is anybody then they'll know we're here!" Scott stated the obvious as they headed up the brick laid drive, although a lot of it was crumbling making it look more like a red gravel driveway.

The door was locked but quickly gave way under a little pressure and they entered. Three skeletal remains lay in various positions, two were collapsed on the floor whilst a smaller third looked as if he or she had been lying down on what was now the remains of a sofa.

"It's almost impossible to describe what it must have been like for them. Everywhere seems to suggest it was incredibly quick." Robyn looked about the room, saddened by the sight.

"Plus, most places appear to have been burnt, probably at the start of whatever happened. Must have been a helluva firestorm, they didn't stand a chance," added Scott as he walked through and worked out the layout of the villa.

"Reminds me of what they found when excavating Pompeii…" muttered Robyn and Scott shrugged as he looked into a side room.

"Hey, at least there's a toilet without having to go up a rickety flight of stairs. No water or paper though." He carried on exploring.

Robyn was in the kitchen but as with everywhere else, nothing had survived that was edible or even recognisable. She entered the bedroom and found Scott in there lying on what should have been a double bed that had collapsed.

"I think we'd be better off on the floor, this is so uncomfortable now the bedding and mattress have mostly disintegrated. Must have been one of those memory foam mattresses."

Together they pushed the remains to one side and did their best to clean up the room, all the while trying to cover their faces to avoid the dust kicked up by their actions.

"At least there's a roof and ceiling. May as well stay here for the time being?" Robyn wondered out loud.

"Well, as the hotel up the road hasn't got any rooms, then I think that's a good idea."

"Ha! Tell you what, let's move the bed to the far side of the window and tilt it up to block it just in case it does rain whilst we're asleep. Might block some of the windowless hole and stop us getting scalded by the rain," she countered and helped Scott stand as they moved the debris of the bed over towards the window alcove, angling it to cover as much of the window as possible.

They then cleared a better spot on the opposite side of the room, closest to the door and settled down with the rucksacks as bumpy pillows.

For a while as the sky turned to twilight outside with its rich reddish orange hues, they didn't say a word, their own thoughts flying around inside their heads.

Without warning Robyn spoke.

"I really hope it was quick for them."

"Say what?"

"Danny and Trina. Regardless of what might have gone on, I hope it was quick and painless."

Robyn lowered her head onto Scott's shoulder.

"Yeah ..." he said quietly. His thoughts turned to Katrina and a tear formed in his left eye, so he wiped it away.

"Do you ..." Robyn started but fell silent.

"Think they were really having an affair?" Scott finished for her. She sat up but looked down at her feet, deep in thought. He continued, "Yes. I'm reasonably sure of it but didn't have any proof."

"Well, I did."

Scott leaned forward and looked back at her in shock. "What? How?"

She looked slowly up at him as if she wished she'd not said anything. "Promise you won't be mad at me?"

"Of course, I could never be mad at you. We're, well, we're like a team, you and I. Aren't we?"

"You could say that," Robyn replied then took his hand. "Last year I found a slip, a receipt in Danny's holiday shorts that he'd forgotten to get rid of. It was a cash receipt in Euros for a room in one of the seaside front hotels in Lagos. The dates and times all coincided with when we went into the interior, one of them was when we visited Silves and looked around the castle and church.

The other was when we ventured further north in search of that archaeological site we never found. You know, we ended up at one of the Baragems instead. In all cases we expected to be gone for several hours whilst they supposedly were on the beach."

Scott was quiet as he took all of this in.

"I didn't have confirmation, but I did suspect it. Trina always seemed a bit *too* eager looking forward to our joint holiday."

"Well, if it's any consolation, so did I…"

They both fell silent and didn't speak any more as the room darkened and Robyn again put her head on Scott's shoulder. He didn't react but together, they fell asleep, each lost in their own thoughts.

#

Robyn stirred wondering what it was that had awoken her, and she could barely see anything as it was so dark. Then she remembered they'd pushed the bed up against the window, although it didn't fully cover the opening.

It happened again as she saw the flash of light illuminate the room briefly and so she listened carefully, counting the seconds.

A roll of distant thunder suggesting the storm was still some way off and she cuddled into Scott who moved slightly in his sleep but didn't wake. She always admired those who could sleep through storms and indeed even envied them that ability.

Despite hating thunder and lightning, she carefully wriggled out from beside him whilst he just seemed to stay in one position, as if he was glued to the wall by his head. She tip toed out of the room and headed to the lounge. It seemed to originally have had large glass doors that opened out to the patio and swimming pool that on initial inspection appeared devoid of water.

The glass in the doors had been shattered and over time was either washed away or so heavily worn it no longer posed a danger to her feet. The swimming pool now had almost a foot of water in it, but she had to admit it wasn't a big pool at all.

She sat on the floor just inside the room and watched the gathering storm as she told herself to face it and beat her fears. After what they had been through so far, it now seemed to her to be daft to be afraid of something like a natural event when for all she and Scott knew, the whole world was now desolate and lifeless.

Now that *was* something to be scared of, she mused then flinched as a flash of light lit up the sky in the distance. The rain came down in fits and starts; for a short while it was just drizzle then a sudden onset of a heavy downpour followed by more consistent, heavy rain.

Another, brighter, flash and she jumped a little as her mind had wandered, but she stayed sitting cross legged, determined to face it out.

She tried to remember the direction and realised the storm had blown in from the Atlantic, hence the rain fell at a slant almost crossways on to the villa and her view.

Apart from the flashes of lightning, she could only hear the rain striking the patio area and splashing in the pool. Well away from her so no chance of getting scalded by the contaminated rain.

For what felt like ages, the storm didn't seem to get any nearer and she surmised it was skirting the coast and probably heading inland into what was once Spain.

Countries…

How vain, humans had been coming up with artificial borders, cutting each other off all through history, yet look at it all now.

Gone.

The rain fell harder, and she retreated further back into the room to watch from a distance but without realising it, sleep caught up with Robyn and she slowly settled down and drifted off into a deep and troubled sleep.

CHAPTER 11: GAME ON...

Daylight, and as Robyn stirred she heard a voice off to one side.

"You OK?"

Scott sat down by her side and looked at her then glanced out through the windowless doors towards the patio and the pool. The day was drab, and the rain was still falling, but steadily now instead of heavily as it was during the storm. Some of the rain had splattered into the room suggesting a change in the wind direction sometime about dawn.

"Yeah. I meant to come back to you, but I wanted to be bold and face the storm. Face my fears, if that doesn't sound too corny!" Robyn said quietly.

"Seems to me like you beat it then as you're still here," he replied and smiled. His positivity struck a chord deep inside her and she touched him on the shoulder.

"You know what? I think you are right. Plus talking about things last night and getting them out in the open ..."

"Robyn, that's all in the past, however long ago that was. I would say we should get on with life but, let's face it, under the current circumstances, that's not saying much is it! I was thinking after I woke up, whilst it is raining I don't think we should risk moving from here for the time being.

Also, we have to face the fact that there is no

food other than the scraps we have left and the thunder last night could have been my stomach rumbling due to the lack of food."

"Ha, yes, you're right about the last bit; well, I'm scared more now of what will happen to us than any silly noises from the sky."

"Who wouldn't be? This is going to sound daft but, I'd rather you promise you won't cook me up and eat my remains if I pop my clogs first and I promise I won't do the same to you."

"Ewww. Perish the thought. Anyway, once our food runs out we'll begin to thin - bit of a drastic way to lose weight but we can last for a few weeks before we get too weak to move. Let's not go there, but ..." She looked suddenly deep in thought as if something had come to her. "Didn't Judith at our holiday villa say her pantry was in an underground cellar?"

"I'm not sure. I think so, why?"

"So far everything on the surface is destroyed, turned to dust or affected by the acid rain. What if something was stored underground? They used to do that before fridges were invented."

Scott's face brightened a little despite the continuing greyness of the sky and the persistent, now turning heavy, downpour. "There's a thought. We can make it back but not if it's raining acid outside. Hopefully the good old Algarve sunshine will return soon. We can backtrack if we can remember the route we've taken."

"Don't know about you but we wandered a bit

and made a few diversions. But if we can get back to the remains of the motorway then follow it until we reach either where we got onto it after we emerged from the cave or follow it until we reach the junction we used to take in order to head into the hills and to the villa."

"Not sure about the last bit." Scott looked at her and she frowned.

"Why?"

"Remember, the bridge over the valley is collapsed."

"Oh bugger, then we'll just have to retrace our steps from there," she said, now feeling determined as they seemed to have a plan.

"When the rain stops."

"When the rain stops," she echoed.

They got up and walked through into the bedroom and sat on the floor next to their rucksacks.

It took a lot of willpower to only take one bite out of the sardine sandwich each and a small lump of Madeira cake whilst carefully catching and keeping any crumbs. Scott grimaced slightly at eating the sandwich as he hated sardines, however, beggars couldn't be choosers, especially under the current circumstances he figured.

They looked at the water bottle that was the stream water then both reached for the half empty bottle of squash and chuckled nervously.

"You too, eh?" Scott offered knowing how much they seemed to always be in tune.

"I know, we have to brave it at some point." Before she could add anything else Scott reached over, twisted the plastic top off and took a drink from the water bottle then recapped it. Robyn looked sternly at him.

"You daft thing. I'm lighter than you, what if I have to carry you?"

"Too late now. Seems quite good, a sort of cleanliness to it but little in the way of taste. I did take a sip from the stream where we filled up after all and I'm still here, so it can't be that bad."

"OK, I'll let you off this one time. Don't do it again. We act and decide as a team."

They sat listening to the rain hitting the roof tiles and fell into quiet, thoughtful, reflective thoughts. They had no idea of how long they sat there although on several occasions they both shuffled several times as their posteriors became numb.

"I spy with my little eye." Scott began and Robyn groaned.

"No, please, not that."

They fell quiet again.

"Something beginning with B," she suddenly said after a few minutes, startling Scott.

"Bed?"

"Yes."

"Something beginning with W," he offered.

"Wall?"

"Yep. How about something beginning with C."

"Cloud!" Robyn said, slightly more excited than

she'd expected.

"NO! Gottcha." Scott announced triumphantly. Robyn gazed about, then face palmed.

"Ceiling?"

"Yes."

"Anyhow, it was my turn as you cheated. How long do you think we can keep this up?" she asked, looking around for more inspiration. "Beginning with I ..."

Now that had Scott puzzled as he looked around the pretty desolate and hardly furnished room. He frowned and spent several minutes looking about but shaking his head. Gradually Robyn's patience began to wear thin.

"Oh for heaven's sake, answer or give in!"

"Charming I'm sure. Now I get to see the real you, eh?"

She slapped him on his arm playfully but gave him such a look as to wither a flower.

"No, I can't see it, give up." He reluctantly gave in.

"Impression."

"WHAT?"

"Look, on the wall to our left, there's an impression of where a painting used to hang."

"Oh for fuck's sake!"

"Ha! Never heard you swear like that before. *Now* who's colours are we seeing?" Robyn asked defiantly.

"Well, I mean. Clever but too clever for me," he replied but for a while he did seem to sink into a quiet little sulk. Robyn stood up and wandered into the front room then around into the kitchen and dining room and kicked aside some of the remains of the table that must have stood there before the four legs had disintegrated.

She headed back out into the front lounge and sat cross legged on the floor, watching the rain fall hard onto the outside patio. Her stomach rumbled and she shook her head knowing there was nothing either of them could do and a tear welled up and dribbled down her right cheek.

Wiping it away she heard padded footsteps and turned to see Scott wander into the lounge, sit next to her and take her hand.

"Sorry. I was being a big kid."

"Well, we were playing a kiddies game so there's your excuse." She looked at the dreary view before them. "When will this rain stop?" she asked in despair.

"When it does, I guess," Scott offered, knowing it was of little help. He stood back up and headed into the other room again but returned shortly with their rucksacks.

"With this cloud cover, we may as well stay in here," he suggested, and Robyn took her rucksack and put it down to lay her head on it.

Despite it being daytime, they both dropped off to sleep.

The rain kept relentlessly falling, oddly, without hissing ...

#

She stirred, something didn't feel right, and she felt hot, sticky and wet.

Wet.

Wet?

Robyn sat bolt upright and realised that her legs and bottom were soaked, and she started prodding Scott hurriedly to wake up.

"Scott. SCOTT!! Wake up your daft bugger, we're being soaked in acid rain!"

Scott stirred then sat up quickly but just as he was about to swear Robyn stopped him.

"Hang on. This is just wet. I'm not burning."

She carefully felt the damp on her legs and noted it was still daylight. There was a small 'stream' that had made its way into the lounge, but she was not in pain. She reached out and gently put her hand into it, ready to pull out instantly, but ...

It was just plain old warmish water. Robyn sighed with relief as did Scott. They both stood and walked over to the patio doors and stepped out feeling the rain with their hands and to their relief, it was simply rainwater, not stinging pain as each drop hit their skin.

The 'stream' was overflowing from the pool which was full due to the incessant rainfall over the last few days.

"Ahh, normally there is a water circulation system and a drain to stop this happening. The drain must be blocked and of course there's no power for any pump to work," Scott offered.

Robyn walked out further into the rain and looked up enjoying the water spill onto and over her hair. She spun around revelling in the wash she was getting; could feel the rain washing away the layers of dust that had been tormenting her since they awoke in the cave several days earlier. She pushed her hands through her hair unknotting it as best she could with glee.

Scott laughed and joined her, getting soaked to the skin. He pulled his shirt off and rubbed the water over his chest much to Robyn's delight as she massaged her arms clean with the rainfall. Without thinking she took off her blouse and revelled in the water falling on her chest and rubbing herself all over, enjoying the feeling.

Scott smirked but now inhibitions were quickly being forgotten as he took off his shorts to reveal his rather skimpy boxers. Robyn did likewise revealing her panties and they both revelled in the rain, becoming absolutely soaked.

Passions stirred.

She took note of it and smiled.

Robyn took off her bra and he removed his pants as they moved closer.

They continued to bask in the rain, but emotions were building as Robyn slipped off her panties.

They closed in and passionately kissed as pent-up emotions finally came to a head and they lay down in the rain on the patio and made love

without a care in the world.
    The rain it kept a falling.
          They no longer cared.

CHAPTER 12: BACK ON THE 'ROAD' AGAIN

Lying there they still enjoyed the feel of the rain as it fell and held hands for a while.

"I've been wanting, hoping, for that for , Robyn said quietly.

"I guess deep down, so have I."

"Guess we were too loyal," she added.

"Unlike the other two ..."

Scott looked over at the pool. Getting up, he helped Robyn to her feet and motioned to the pool and then let go of her hand and dived in. She quickly followed and soon they were laughing, splashing water at each other and for what seemed like just a few minutes, but was at least an hour they cavorted in the pool, enjoying each other's company.

So much so they didn't notice it stop raining. Scott wiped the water from his eyes and looked at Robyn, swam up to her and they gently hugged.

"Well, it's just you and me kiddo!"

"Oh, you do say the nicest things Sir Galahad."

"We could literally be the only boy in the world and you the only girl."

"Well, that brings us back down to earth again, doesn't it!" she retorted but splashed him in the face then turned and headed for the shallow end, laughing.

As she lifted herself out of the pool he just

floated there, enjoying the view as she turned, put her hands on her shapely hips and looked at him intently.

"Well, you coming out now? Have you not noticed the sun has come out but it's also late afternoon?"

He took his eyes away from her and noted she was right, swam up to the shallow end then hauled himself out.

She watched him and mentally compared him with Danny but then pushed thoughts of her husband out of her mind, knowing he was dead. Time to move on, Robyn thought to herself.

"I think it best if we stay outside but in the shade so we can dry off and if we put our clothes on the wall over there then they may dry quicker. I wouldn't want to spend all night au naturel as I reckon we'd catch our deaths of cold."

"Good thinking. Err, does this mean we're an item now?" Scott asked lamely.

"Oh Scott! Really? What a daft thing to say. We're likely the only ones left! Have you *seen* anyone else?"

Scott just shook his head but inwardly smiled. They arranged their clothes to catch the sun but being naked, could feel the rays burning their skin, so quickly headed back into the shade of the lounge wall and sat down.

Scott snuggled into Robyn, and they cuddled, happy and for the first time unabashed since they had emerged into this strange new world.

"You know, joking apart, even if we are the only ones left, how could we repopulate our world when there's nothing to eat."

"Way to go Scott, destroy the mood! But, well, I know you are right. I simply don't have an answer." There was a silence for several minutes as they both contemplated their bleak future, despite finally admitting their feelings for each other.

Feelings don't feed people, mused Robyn as she lay her head on Scott's shoulder.

"You know, I reckon you are right. Head back to our holiday villa and see if there is any chance anything edible survived. I doubt any of our things survived whatever happened on the surface whilst we were trapped underground, but if the pantry cellar is intact it may be our last hope?"

"No point now as it must be into evening time as the sun is even lower now. We'll set off in the morning then we can keep a look out for any approaching storms. I suspect that anything coming from the heart of the continent may be acidic whilst rain from storms from the Atlantic may be safer for us."

"Why is that?" he asked wondering about the different storms.

"Evaporation from the sea leaves the salt behind then falls as fresh water but anything inland may have contaminants, you know, water interacting directly with certain rocks, the remains of any nuclear or indeed any industrial complexes. Of which, let's face it, there were loads worldwide."

"Charming. Cheerful buggers aren't we!"

"We're faced with the harshest of realities. I noticed that the latest storm came from out in the Atlantic rather from inland so it's my best guess concerning why it wasn't acidic.

Anyhow, I'm dry and beginning to get a chill." Robyn stood up and Scott admired her form as she went into the late evening sunshine and checked the clothes. "Yep, all dry. Here you go with your fancy boxers." She picked up and chucked his shirt, pants and shorts over then brought hers over too and began to dress. "Ooo, nice and warm too. We may as well head indoors and snuggle down."

"You do say the nicest thing. But to be fair, after all our exertions, I'm bushed and worst of all, starving!"

Robyn could only agree, held him by his upper arm and they wandered inside, picked their rucksacks up and headed back into the original bedroom. Using the wind-up torch, they looked at their dwindling supplies and took a bite each out of the last but one sandwich then carefully put it away. A quick gulp each from the water bottle then they settled down for the night, still hungry.

#

Scott slowly opened his eyes and looked around the gently illuminated room. Robyn was curled up fast asleep, so he carefully slid away and stood up wondering what had awoken him.

It didn't feel like they'd been asleep for too long and he had no way to tell the time, but the room was clearly illuminated. He wandered back down the hallway to the lounge and noted how bright it seemed, so he wandered over to the patio doors and looked out.

The almost full moon was just above the horizon, looking slightly yellowish but flooding the land with its second-hand sunlight. Scott smiled at something that was at least familiar from his past. He remembered Danny was into space exploration and often pointed out the moon and some of its basic features. The dark seas didn't seem quite as obvious as Danny had said they were.

He remembered they weren't actually seas but solidified dark lava filling huge asteroid basins, or something like that. Names handed down over centuries from people who only had their own eyes to view it by and thought they could see seas on the moon.

He heard something and spun round only to see Robyn sleepily come up to him.

"You OK hun?"

"Yes, moonlight awoke me."

Robyn looked out and up at it and sighed. "Well at least that still comes up. Almost banishes the night doesn't it!"

Scott looked thoughtful and frowned.

"You know, that might be a better plan. Go tonight whilst the moon is up, and we can see where we're going and still keep an eye out for any storms that may spring up."

Robyn was now fully awake and nodded in agreement. "No sunburn to worry about and if we are roughly heading north then between the two of us we can keep an eye out for storm clouds."

"OK, let's go then, no time to dilly dally as they used to say." Scott picked up his rucksack and looked at her.

"Seems like a long time ago and in a different place and time," sighed Robyn as she grabbed hers and together they walked out through the lounge, onto the patio, took a final look back at their short-lived temporary home, then headed down the driveway and out onto the road.

#

They walked along it for a while then found a turning heading roughly north that they suspected might lead back up to the motorway. All the time, however, they were quiet and kept their thoughts to themselves, concentrating their energy on walking as well as ignoring the pangs of hunger that were gradually increasing along with the slight chill in the air.

Robyn suddenly broke the stillness of the night.

"You know, apart from our footsteps and a

slight sound from the breeze, it's really, really quiet without any form of life or even sounds of civilisation."

"Unnerving if you ask me. It's like those programmes that talked about sensory deprivation and how it can send some people mad," Scott mused out loud.

"I think Danny and Katrina sometimes thought we were mad to go on holiday yet never seem to stop to rest, always out exploring." Robyn said.

"Hah! Trina sometimes asked me why I didn't like sunbathing despite me having skin that burns like pork crackling! I always wondered how someone could go on holiday to such a wonderful place as the Algarve and not explore the local countryside and sights."

"Yeah, Danny sort of hinted at that about sitting out in the sun. I didn't mind on the odd occasion, but that's why we seemed to gel, I mean going off to enjoy the sights."

Scott went quiet for a few minutes, lost in his own thoughts, as they began to walk up the gentle incline of the road. He looked about but there were few houses or villas now, so they were definitely out of the suburbs of Portimao but the slight hill ahead of them blocked their view northwards.

"You remember who it was that suggested we go off on our own to explore?" he asked, teasingly to Robyn who shrugged.

"Not really, was a few years back now, not long after we began to come to the Algarve."

"Trina."

"Really? Not one of us then? I can't remember."

"I do, we were all lying out on our hire beds over at Albufeira. I got bored and suggested walking along a nearby beach and you thought it was a good idea but the other two were not impressed. Then Trina said, 'Go on then, off you go the pair of you and we'll stay here and soak up the sun in peace'.

Later in the nightclub we'd been joking about how it had been refreshing to walk along admiring the views and Trina remembered it the next morning at breakfast."

"Oh, I remember the beach walk now, you admired the topless brunette if I remember the right one."

"Err, well, can I help it if someone puts them on show. Anyhow, reckon they were fake or botox'ed!"

Robyn laughed out loud as they reached the top of the rise and they stopped to look about.

"You can't say that about me, can you," she teased as Scott looked at her and raised his eyebrows admiringly.

"No, you certainly can't."

The moonlit landscape had a surreal aspect but a bright star over in the east caught Robyn's attention.

"Eyh up, what's that?" she pointed towards it and Scott followed her pointing finger.

"Could be a planet, Jupiter or maybe Venus. Danny would know, you know what he's like on this. It is pretty bright. Venus is my guess." He looked southwards. "Oh, that's sort of pretty."

Robyn turned; the moon was high up illuminating the sea. Under any other circumstances she'd have got her smart phone out but as she was about to do so she remembered it was dead.

Then she spotted it.

A slow-moving dot of light silently rising in the west, passing southwards below the moon but then fading from view.

Scott had seen it too.

"Satellite. Guess even after a long time there would still be a few still left orbiting up there. Wish I'd taken more notice of Danny now when he talked about these things."

"Yes, he did know his stuff and was a member of some London based group named after Sherlock Holmes or something like that. Anyone in the space station might have survived if it was a nuclear war, but there'd be nothing to return to so I bet they were stranded up there. Poor sods. I think I'd rather go quickly than linger about in space orbiting a dead world or indeed being stranded on the surface ..."

"Like we are?"

Robyn looked at Scott as the comment hit home, but didn't say anything, just shrugged.

Scott fished his binoculars out, looked at the moon, then at the bright star before looking towards the northern horizon.

"I think we're not far from the motorway so perhaps just a few kilometres from the villa. We should crack on as Danny always said that when the moon was generally in the south it was halfway across the sky, so I reckon that gives us enough time to get there before daybreak."

Robyn took the binoculars, looked around and finished on the bright star.

"Venus. Danny said that in binoculars you could see some of Jupiter's moons either side of it and I can't see any. OK, let's get going then. Lead on love, no time to waste."

CHAPTER 13: SECOND ARRIVAL

For the next hour or so they joined and followed the remains of the motorway, going round some of the crash debris that was still left, usually from large vehicles that took longer to erode.

They missed where they had originally joined it a few days earlier, but came across the abrupt end as the motorway began to span the valley.

Scrambling down the hillside Scott suddenly spotted something on the other side of the valley further up northwards.

"Is that what I think it is?"

Robyn still had the binoculars and brought them up to see. "Yep, I can just see the cave entrance. It's quite small but with the landscape so desolate it stands out a mile."

Encouraged, they continued down the slope then came across the stream at the valley floor and, working their way along it, came to the spot where they'd stopped before.

"This is where we filled up my litre bottle with water. The stream was okay then so guess we ought to top up our water supply?" Scott looked questioningly at Robyn who sat down next to the flowing water and carefully put her finger in. She smiled.

"Not acidic. Seems safe enough and let's face it we don't know if there is any other source of water nearer the villa as I didn't take much notice when we were there."

Scott took his bottle out of the rucksack he was carrying and filled it up, being careful not to get any sediment mixed up in it.

"What with the acid rain, I am still surprised the stream is okay to drink," he muttered. Robyn looked about as she thought more about the drinkable stream.

"I wonder if it actually starts from an underground source. Perhaps the water gets filtered enough or, or maybe as we're near the coast there are more storms coming in from the Atlantic, so most of the time it does fall as relatively fresh clean water. We just happened to have bad luck when the storms came from inland when we emerged from the lower cave entrance."

"I'm just glad we have at least got a water supply."

"Yeah, small mercies and all that," she replied looking around. They surveyed the hillside and spotted the faint remains of the path they had followed just a few days earlier. Together they set off back up towards the cave.

They reached the place where the skeletal remains of their companions lay but were now even more scattered due to the recent storms. They stopped and lowered their heads in respect.

"Don't know about you but I think I'd like to try to give them some sort of burial. There's a hollow over there. Shall we place the bones in it and cover them with rocks?" Scott suggested and Robyn nodded without saying a word. She immediately began to pick up the bones trying not to think that they were once their partners.

Twenty minutes later they looked at the small mound with tears in their eyes as they again uttered silent prayers for Danny and Katrina.

They set off back up the hill in silence, reached the cave and Scott pointed to one side at the faint path and, without prompting, followed it.

Reaching the rather flat top of the hill they looked around and Robyn nodded towards the moon which was now lower in the western sky.

"Rises in the east, sets in the west. Reckon we've got an hour or two at most, so guess we ought to crack on?" she said knowing that Scott wouldn't disagree with her. Silently, he nodded, and they headed off across the top of the hill before stopping, looking down at the other side of the valley towards their destination.

"You know, it took longer to climb up here because we couldn't come straight up as we'd have been trespassing through that farmer's orchard. But we don't have to zigzag our way now, we can just go straight down the hill," he observed.

"Yes, I see it now, there's a faint track that leads roughly down straight towards his home, or what's left of it. Must have been his route to the top to check on his goats. It'll cut down our journey time really well." She didn't wait but set off with Scott quick to follow.

They pushed past a skeleton of what looked to be a dog, then a little further towards the house there was a human skeleton, presumably the farmer. Carrying on there was little left of the house and there were signs of several eroded vehicles, one looked as if it might have once been a tractor whilst the other may have been a small car. Both were just mounds of corroded metal and what was left of any plastic mouldings after the acid rain had done its work.

They found the original road that they had taken regularly down to head to the coast, heavily pockmarked and weather worn; they trudged along it for the next mile or so closing in on their original villa.

They reached what once was quite a magnificent walled entrance, probably for one of the richer locals and curiosity got the better of them as they pushed past the remains of the metal gate and entered the grounds. The villa was collapsed in on itself which didn't bode well for their own holiday villa, just another couple of miles away according to Robyn's calculations.

To one side, through what must have been a walled garden, they spotted something that looked like it had been a large pond, the vegetation, like everything else, was missing although there was some water in one spot. Scott almost stepped in to take a look but stopped suddenly as he sniffed the air.

"Nope, I reckon this is acidic as I can get a whiff

of something sharp coming from it. You wouldn't want to drink that I can tell you," he looked back and up at Robyn.

"Well, no shit Sherlock! The only water that could have been collected would be from the storms and my guess is that we were lucky with the stream. Definitely must be from an aquifer deep down which would at least be filtered, whereas water collected like this is more likely to be acidic as you say. Glad we filled up at the stream but it does seem to suggest we will have to trek back and forth to replenish the water supplies."

Robyn looked around and realised the moon was now behind the hills and twilight was almost on them. "Not long now to sunrise so we'd best get moving."

Scott didn't need to be told.

#

Things came flooding back to them as they reached the top of the last hill and there in front was the entrance to Judith's holiday villa complex.

Or at least what was left of it at first glance.

Dawn was breaking upon the landscape; the moon was nowhere to be seen and the landscape was now almost fully illuminated. The tired pair trudged through the wide-open entrance and were relieved to see much of the villa was actually standing, a side complex was in poorer shape but it was refreshing to their eyes. Not so what appeared to be several rusted mounds, the shapes of cars.

"Guess the hire companies won't be wanting them back now ..." muttered Scott as they walked past the remains. Reaching the path and what should have been the gate to the side entrance where Judith had originally taken them, they wandered around and found their part of the villa largely intact, but with some clear holes in the roof and some tiles missing.

Inside was a mess and clearly at some stage the acid rain had penetrated as their rooms were a jumble of eroded remains of the wardrobe, bed and what should have been their possessions. All utterly useless and barely recognisable as they all bore the sign of having been in an inferno.

Tired, they wandered across the courtyard to Judith's home and trying the door, the handle came away in their hands and the door disintegrated, clattering to the ground, not that anyone would have heard them or been bothered by it.

Looking inside they found a spot that seemed it would offer some protection if a storm brewed and they collapsed to the ground, snuggled up and was almost instantly asleep from their travels.

The sun traversed the sky in its great arc as the earth turned and finally about mid-afternoon Scott came awake and turned to Robyn.

"You OK love?"

She stirred and sat up leaning on one elbow as she cleared her head. "What?"

"I heard you cough so just checking you are

OK?"

"I didn't cough. Wasn't me."

"Yeah you did, must have been in your sleep but there was a definite cough. It woke me up."

"Seriously Scott, I can't rememb …" She was cut short as they both heard the coughing fit in the distance, and they froze staring at each other in shock.

"There's, there's someone *alive and here*! *Judith*?" Robyn whispered and they both got to their feet and edged towards the remains of the door.

Typical, all was now quiet apart from a gentle breeze whistling through the broken tiles of the roof.

Then they heard it again.

They turned their heads almost in synchrony with each other; at any other time it would have looked comical, but not now.

"*Cough.*

Splutter, Cough."

Scott listened then indicated off to their right and whispered in Robyn's ear. "Sounds like it's coming from the small cottage Judith said she had almost got ready for the season but had a setback with."

They slowly crept along the rough path and down a few steps towards the detached cottage at the far edge of the property whilst keeping a sharp eye on the open doorway.

Reaching it, they gingerly poked their heads in

and stood in utter shock.

Danny and Katrina were a sorry sight, curled up in one corner looking terrible with hardly any hair, badly damaged clothes and peeling red raw skin exposed on their faces shoulders, legs and hands.

Recovering their composure, Robyn and Scott dashed into the room and knelt carefully next to their respective partners as they tried to hold back the tears.

"Oh my god, sweetheart, what, dear god, what happened to you both?" Robyn held Danny's head gently in her hands as she tried to support him to sit up. He couldn't seem to speak, and she realised his eyes were clouded over.

He was blind.

Katrina was in only a slightly better shape as Scott held her gingerly in his arms.

"We thought, we thought you were both buried alive in the cave fall." Katrina stuttered.

"No love, we managed to find a different way out only to discover the devastation. But what happened to you both, how did you survive?"

"I. I don't know how. Danny, Danny and I, I think we got radiation poisoning or something like that.

He drank water from a pool as we were so thirsty, but it burned his mouth and insides. I don't think he'll make it. The rain. The rain it's like acid and we both got drenched. It was awful. Scalding. I still had my sun hat, but he'd lost his and it dribbled into his eyes, blinding him.

Why has this all happened to us? Where is everybody?" she cried.

Danny tried to say something but coughed and brought up blood and what could only be bits of his oesophagus. Robyn was struggling holding back the tears as she cradled him.

Scott brought out their water bottle and gave Katrina a sip of water then handed it to Robyn but on the first gulp of water Danny threw up and it was obvious he didn't have much time left.

Danny reached out towards Katrina who wriggled over to him and took him by the hand and although he tried to say something Katrina understood and looked at Scott then Robyn.

"We, we have to tell you something. We're sorry. We never meant it to happen, but things got out of hand. Before all this, we were having an affair every holiday we had in the Algarve, and it was wrong. We're so, so sorry."

Robyn jumped in before Scott could say anything.

"Hey, it's OK love. We were too. So don't you two feel guilty as we were all at it. I'm sorry too and I'm sure Scott is too, right Scott?" she gave him a sideways look that could have turned him to stone.

"Yes, we were going to tell you this holiday but couldn't bear to."

Katrina tried to laugh but she too began to cough, but at least there was no sign of blood.

"You two make lousy liars you know. Have you

anything to eat? We've not had anything for the last few days as Danny didn't pick up his rucksack before we dived into the cave for safety."

Robyn opened hers up and, looking at Scott who nodded in agreement, she broke off a small chunk from the last sandwich and brought it up to Katrina's lips who readily devoured it then indicated for water.

A few moments later and she violently threw it all up, this time with blood and she began to shake uncontrollably. Scott held her as best he could until she settled down, but it was now clear neither of their partners were going to survive.

"Trina? Trina?" he called to her gently. She came too and seemed to have settled down.

"How did you two survive? We found two bodies further down the hillside from the cave and assumed they were you," he said gently.

Katrina managed to pull herself up into a roughly sitting position whilst leaning into Scott and thought for a moment or two.

"Ahh, that's sad, it must be the two ladies that were about an hour or so behind us on the walk. We met them, their names are, or were, Sammy and Gail. Gail looked so meek and mild too. They'd not long carried on down the trail as they realised they'd be crowding us at the cave entrance. Poor sods. Wouldn't have stood a chance." Katrina looked lost in her thoughts whilst Danny was asleep in Robyn's arms, and she didn't want to disturb him.

Scott cuddled Katrina as best he could, noting her wince due to the acid burns on her arms and legs.

"Trina. Trina, can you tell us what happened to you two once we were in the cave?"

"Yeah, not much to say but will try to get it right."

She took a breath and sank her head into Scott's chest as she began to recount how they'd survived.

CHAPTER 14: AGAINST THE ODDS

They looked on in horror as the smoke and flames pushed into the cave entrance. Danny desperately clawed at the spot where Robyn had said earlier that there was another tunnel leading down deeper into the cave, but now they discovered to their horror it had been blocked, probably with the tremor they'd felt earlier.

Katrina reached into her rucksack and pulled out the wind up torch that Judith had given her, not really expecting to have any use for it. Frantically looking round, she grabbed Danny by the shorts to get his attention then scrambled further along the cave wall to a smaller 'hole' for want of a better word.

They dug, panic rising as they could feel the heat building, until part of the hole sides gave way and they finally wriggled through, not knowing what to expect.

Slumping down on top of each other, Danny wriggled back up and started pushing soil and rocks to block the hole and Katrina lodged the torch and joined in, finally sealing it up. In the close confines as motes of dust floated through the air in the torchlight, Danny settled down, exhausted.

"It might hold. Gawd, I hope it does!"

Katrina moved the torchlight around only for

them to see they were in a small cavern roughly three metres wide and less than a metre and a half high but with no other sign of an exit.

A dead end.

But what caught their attention was the eerie purplish glow emanating from dozens of crystals scattered, lodged in the wall and ceiling and very quickly they both succumbed to a deep sleep.

#

"Trina. Trina? You there?" Danny awoke to find he couldn't open his eyes but could feel Katrina next to him. She grumbled something, turned over in the dark and banged her head against his and they both swore. It was a bit muffled as they began to realise their lips were sore but had at least come apart with the accidental head butt.

"I can taste blood on my lips, and they hurt like hell! What happened?" she asked groggily. "I can't open my eyes - what the hell?"

Danny could be heard rummaging around in the only rucksack they had, then made a triumphant gruff sound.

"Gottcha! Found the water bottle. Might work as it feels like my eyes are gunged up with sleep. We've got to have been here quite a few hours for that to happen." He felt for his eyes then brought up the bottle and squirted some of its contents onto his eyes but winced and swore. "Bloody orange squash! Wrong bottle!"

But it did the trick and although they were smarting, he opened his eyes only to realise it was pitch black. He felt about on the ground and found the wind-up torch still lodged in the cave floor, hoping it was working. Winding it up, the small cave was flooded with light, making him blink as his eyes adjusted to the surreal view and he looked into the rucksack to find the water bottle.

He splashed the water into Katrina's eyes, she struggled, then finally pried them open and blinked against the glare of the light from the torch.

She coughed in the dusty atmosphere and looked at Danny, scared out of her wits.

"What do you think happened?"

"Dunno. Worst case, nuclear war? Perhaps it was something localised and we're just unlucky? I really don't know."

He reached into his shorts pocket and fished out his smartphone, but it was dead, lifeless.

"Odd, it had a decent charge on it; nothing. I'll try rebooting it."

After several attempts, it was clear the battery was dead and Katrina checked hers too to find the same problem.

"This is freaking me out," she said shaking her head. "Both phones are dead? Coincidence? I'm all covered in dust as are you, so just how long have we been in here for?"

"Guess we must have been out cold for at least a few days. Explains the dustiness and dead batteries."

And the gunged up eyes and sore lips."

"True."

"That other tunnel looked pretty bad, it must have caved in, trapping them. I don't think Scott and Robyn made it." Danny said quietly as Katrina took him gently by the arm.

"Don't think that! I know my Scott would never give in and neither would your Robyn. Let's see if we can dig our way back out and hope that someone survived out there and is looking for us."

Danny nodded and looked at her warmly. "Glad one of us is thinking straight."

He turned and they both crawled up to where they'd blocked up the tunnel entrance.

After almost an hour they finally pushed a hand though into the upper cave and were relieved to see light flood into it. They quickly expanded the hole until they could wriggle out, one at a time. Danny went first, much to the wry enjoyment of Katrina who made sure she had the torch looking straight at his backside. She followed and they headed to the entrance and looked out.

Shock.

One way to describe how they felt on seeing the barren desolate landscape.

"Where's the trees, grass, and vegetation?" muttered Katrina as they instinctively held hands looking at the awful view before them.

"This is wrong. We'd best see if we can dig out the other collapsed tunnel and find Robyn and

Scott."

They headed back inside but on inspection it was clear the roof had collapsed in with rocks and debris that only a JCB would be able to shift.

Stunned and lost for words they headed back outside and sat on the ground disconsolate.

"If we can't get in…"

"They can't have survived, probably buried alive. Oh, it's awful!" Katrina broke down in tears quickly joined by Danny as they tried to console each other, knowing they'd never see their other halves again.

They sat for several minutes then became aware that the sky was clear, and the sun was hot, and they had no sunscreen.

"Damn! I've remembered, the sunscreen was in my rucksack, and I didn't manage to grab it before the disaster. It must be out here somewhere," Danny said.

He stood and began looking around. He spotted the remains of the porta chairs they'd seemingly only sat in a few hours earlier yet it must now have been days ago. As he touched them, they fell apart. Katrina pointed at something a little further on and went over, picing it up only for Danny's rucksack to disintegrate into fragments and the contents likewise.

Open mouthed, Katrina looked at Danny in disbelief.

"This, this can't be right. What could have done this?"

Danny just looked on in shock, then realised something.

"Hey Trina. What's up with the hair?"

She looked at him puzzled. "C'mon, we've been stuck in a cave for a few days so give a girl a break won't ya!"

"No, I mean…" he gently reached up and pulled a handful of hair away as Katrina looked on in shock. She did the same to him and they both stood looking at the clumps of each other's hair, with dawning realisation of what it entailed.

"They really did it didn't they? Blew up the world with nuclear weapons. The stupid idiots! Killed us all!" she said and sat down on the ground feeling hollow and lost.

"I never thought they'd be so dumb as to actually do it," he said quietly as he took in the ramifications of their hair loss, sitting down next to her, not knowing what to say or do.

They wallowed in self-pity for an hour or so, when Katrina realised her skin was itching.

Without sunscreen to put on it she noted it was turning bright red, along with flakes of skin beginning to peel away.

"Danny, whatever we do we had best find some sort of shelter other than this barren cave and see if we can find any survivors. Surely we can't be the only ones?"

"Look around. It's worse than any of the disaster movies I used to watch. No vegetation at all spells disaster in my book. You're right about us finding shelter though as I can feel my skin shrieking at me to get under cover."

Danny stood up and held out a hand to Katrina who took it and joined him. They looked about and back along where they thought they'd originally walked as a foursome to find the cave system.

Reaching the flat top of the hill they again surveyed the barren landscape and Danny just pointed at the distant ruins of Portimao and then gasped at how far out the sea appeared to be and shook his head in disbelief.

"Let's head back to our villa and on the way keep a look out for survivors. Didn't we pass a few other houses and villas when we came this way to find the caves?"

"Yes, I think there's a farmer's home and some shelter, so we'd best see if anyone is there and take shelter from this sun. I'm getting thirsty." Katrina swung her rucksack around to her front and unzipped the top to find the water bottle. She took it out then stared at the tiny amount swilling around at the bottom as Danny looked at it in surprise.

"Shit. I must have shaken more over your eyes than I thought. Never mind, we should be able to fill up at the farmer's house, if he's still alive."

They headed off in the direction they thought was right until Danny realised they no longer needed to follow a path and instead headed directly across the hilltop and looked down towards where he suspected the farmer's house was.

Spotting it they set off, but it soon became apparent it was in a terrible state, then they spotted something that struck home how serious their situation might be and that they were likely to be the lucky ones.

Two skeletons, one of a person and the other what looked like a dog. They skirted round them and on reaching the remains of the house it was clear that there was little left. It had been poorly built in the first place, but it still struck them that the house shouldn't be in such bad condition after the few days they'd been stuck in the cave.

There was no signs of any explosions, no craters, nothing to indicate a blast wave had hit it. Simply put, it looked like it had collapsed due to age, weathering and scorch marks and they remembered the firestorm they saw which had prompted them to seek shelter in the cave in the first place.

There was a stone built small hut, for want of a better word, and fortunately most of its roof was still intact. They did a quick search for a kitchen in the remains of the house but to no avail, so there was no water. With the sun still beating down on them it was time to take shelter in the hut.

Signs of tools and possible tractor parts littered the floor, so they had to be careful, but finally they sat down in the shade where at least the heat was no longer intense as they fell into a deep sleep.

Katrina suddenly awoke and, as she gathered

her thoughts, it was apparent they had been asleep for several hours. Danny was snoring next to her, sprawled out and in the weak light she became aware that the sun had to be quite low and close to setting.

She had to admit as she watched Danny's chest gently move up and down as he breathed, she didn't feel at all well and was still very tired. They hadn't exactly overexerted themselves and it was really only a short journey from the cave to the farmer's house, so it just didn't feel right.

Danny stirred and sat up, rubbed the sleep out of his eyes and looked about. Katrina saw him remember what had happened and he turned to her looking tired and saddened.

"I thought it was a dream," he said a little lamely, but she just put her arm around him and squeezed gently.

"Yeah. Wish it was. Anyhow, sun must be getting low. Perhaps time to head off back to our villa and see what state it's in and if Judith survived."

They stood and ventured out to find the sun was actually still well up but the whole sky was clouding over from the north, with dark menacing clouds blotting out the blue sky.

"This may sound daft, but I'd welcome some rain, would be like a shower and might get rid of some of this caked on dust," suggested Danny as Katrina shrugged looking as if she agreed.

"Well, come on then. There's the road up ahead

we came down on, so if we follow that back, then take a left turning, we won't be long before we're at the villa, maybe an hour or two at most?"

They set off as the sky changed with the clouds seemingly thinning out then becoming thick and heavy again. Danny was getting thirsty and rued using all the water up, indeed on checking he'd also wasted the orange squash when he'd accidentally thought it was water hoping to clear his eyes back in the cave.

Rain would at least be a pleasant distraction and he wondered about holding his cupped hands out in the hope of catching some to drink.

It didn't rain as they trudged up the road, but the sky grew dark and heavy with potential for a downpour. A flash of lightning caught them by surprise, then a sharp peal of thunder mere seconds later suggested it was only a few miles away.

Then the heavens opened up.

Instinctively Danny looked up into the sky to catch the drops to satiate his thirst and cupped his hands and gulped down the water, but in an instant his tongue and mouth were burning as Katrina too screamed with pain.

"Christ! It's like acid!" she shouted and put her sunhat on for some limited protection. Danny was stumbling along as the downpour turned into a torrent and they could feel their exposed skin burning with each drop's impact. Danny was shouting now and almost screaming as they both ran along the road trying to find shelter, but the rain was dripping down from his head into his eyes, and he was writhing in agony as his eyeballs were scalded.

Katrina grabbed him by the waist and spotting a driveway, she pushed Danny along, guiding him as he cried out in pain. She too began to feel the acidic water soak through her flimsy clothes and begin to burn her skin. They stumbled up to a door, but it was stuck fast so they staggered around until they found a porchway that gave some shelter from the rain.

They slumped to the ground as she held Danny trying to soothe him as their bodies stung from their wet clothes. She quickly tore them off then undressed Danny and put them to one side as they sheltered not knowing for how long the ordeal would continue.

It felt like the end of the world and there was nothing more they could do as Danny continued to cry out in agony, trying desperately to rub his eyes as Katrina tried to stop him doing any more damage to them.

#

A strong breeze developed, and night fell as they shivered in the porch as the clouds departed and the stars came out. Danny had settled a little but still whimpered and still tried to rub his eyes.

Katrina stopped him as kindly as she could.

She stood up and stretched and, after soothing him, she wandered around until she found a patio door that she was able to push open. Although dusty and in a terrible state, nonetheless there was a roof, so she did her best and managed to help Danny stagger to the room before collapsing into a heap, exhausted. They huddled on the floor against a wall and tried to keep each other warm.

It was a fitful night with little in the way of sleep, but Katrina knew they would have to move on and try to get to their holiday villa in the perhaps vain hope that more of it was still standing and that there may well be fresh water.

Danny kept coughing and a couple of times he brought up blood which didn't bode well for her companion and lover.

Daybreak and a quick search of the villa showed that everything seemed to have just disintegrated and once again there was no fresh running water in the taps. She ..."

Robyn interrupted Katrina as she was recounting their story.

"I wonder if you were at the villa we found on our way back up here. Had a large pool outside the patio doors."

Katrina shook her head.

"There was no pool at this one. I'm nearly finished anyway."

As Danny seemed to swim in and out of consciousness, she continued with their side of the story.

That morning the hot sun dried out their clothes and Katrina helped Danny to get dressed but found he could barely talk. A look in his mouth showed it was a scalded mess, red and in places raw and bloody.

They headed out back onto the road, ignoring the hot sun and hoping to get to the holiday villa as soon as they could. It took another two hours before they finally stumbled onto the driveway and made their way to their original rooms only to find the roof had fallen in.

Sitting Danny down in the shade of one of the walls, Katrina wandered around then noted the unused semi-detached part of the villa situated around the back of the holiday centre and she was relieved it appeared reasonably intact.

She helped Danny stumble round and into it before leaving him fitfully sleeping as she scouted the villa for any fresh water.

There was none. The last thing she remembered was falling asleep then waking to a coughing fit and finding Danny having periodic convulsions. She tried to feed him with the last sandwich she had left in her rucksack, but he threw it up with blood mixed in the vomit making her fear for the worst as he began coughing continuously.

Then she heard voices and was shocked to see Scott and Robyn looking in on them.

The relief of seeing them was almost overwhelming.

"So that's it. That's how we ended up here and in such a state," concluded Katrina.

She suddenly had a bad coughing fit, Scott handed her his last tissue; held her gently and noted she too had blood in her tissue which didn't bode well. Danny was still shivering then went into a violent series of convulsions, coughing blood until he subsided and became still. Robyn was still holding him in her arms and stared in horror with a dawning realisation.

She felt for his pulse.

Nothing. She checked again in several of the places she had been shown once when she was one of the few girls in the boy scouts.

Nothing.

She buried her head into his chest and began sobbing but as Scott tried to move to touch her for support Katrina held him back and whispered.

"Let her grieve, she loved him as did I and I'm so sorry you had to find out like this." She coughed and seemed to fade out a little before regaining her composure. "Look after Robyn, promise me you will look after her. You need each other and make a great couple. You will need each other like never before if you two are going to survive." She again coughed and seemed to become even paler than before.

"No, you're not going to give in Katrina. You

can't. I, I love you and we were always good for each other. Please, hold on. We'll find someone, somehow."

"Ever the optimist. Don't kid yourself. We were higher up in the cave system, closer to the surface and despite whatever it was that preserved us, it didn't fully protect us like it seems to have done for you two.

I, I'm tired, let me sleep."

Scott watched her close her eyes and immediately felt for her pulse and took in a deep breath on finding it, weak but still there.

The foursome stayed there into and through the night as Robyn slowly came to terms with the loss of Danny. Scott held Katrina in his arms, gently rocking her and hoping against all hope for a miracle.

Daybreak came and Robyn awoke with cramp in her arms from holding Danny's body so tightly, then Scott stirred, and he was suddenly wide awake.

He felt for a pulse then began to sob, knowing that Katrina had succumbed in the night. Robyn gently put her hand on his shoulder, and he held it as they spent the rest of the day just sitting with their lost partners, not wishing to accept reality.

They'd lost them for a second time.

Their own plight no longer mattered.

CHAPTER 15: DOWNHILL

Two days passed and finally they laid the bodies out in the room they had found them in and Robyn and Scott quietly, sombrely, walked back up to what had been their shared accommodation and sat down on the tiled floor ,not knowing what to do next.

Scott looked into their rucksack and pulled out the remaining last half of the ham and cheese sandwich and examined it.

A small amount of green mould had appeared at one corner. He picked it off, broke the sandwich into two equal halves and handed one piece to Robyn. She started to turn it away but the look on Scott's face changed her mind.

"This is it Robyn, our last meal. May as well get it over and done with, otherwise tomorrow it will be completely green and inedible."

"I don't really want it," she replied almost in a whisper.

"Look, I get it. How do you think I feel eh? But it's no help to their memories if you don't eat. Let's make it a last meal to remember them by and hope to high heaven that somehow, by some miracle, we do find something to eat. But you're not eating me bits if it gets to that, agreed?"

That last comment did bring a little smile to Robyn's tired face.

"Trust you to think like that." Robyn suddenly grabbed and hugged him tightly.

"Thank you for being the light at the end of the tunnel. I always loved your humorous quips, the few that there were always made me smile regardless of what was going on."

"We're back to being the only ones again, so we have to look after each other until we are too weak to carry on," he said quietly.

"I know."

They fell silent as they ate the final remains of the sandwich. Robyn wiped her face. "Pass us the water bottle." He did so, and she drank a little, knowing that she had become dehydrated, but he saw there was only a small amount left.

"Looks like we'll have to fetch some more." Scott said.

"I'll go when it's dark and the moon comes up, now I know the way I can get to the stream, fill up and be back within ninety minutes to an hour I reckon."

"No way. I'm not staying here by myself. We stick together from now on. Agreed?"

She smiled meekly at him knowing there was no point to arguing with him.

"We should look in Trina's rucksack and take her water bottles too," suggested Scott but was surprised at the answer.

"No. We can't." Robyn seemed quite forthright in her stance.

"Why ever not?"

"Think about what she said and the fact they've both died. It was radiation poisoning.

Fallout. We were much deeper and somehow have escaped the worst but, but they didn't.

And neither would her rucksack either. We can't risk using it or anything from it just in case."

"I didn't think of it like that," Scott said quietly as he thought back to what Trina had told them. "Glad you're the sensible one of us. I'd have just fetched it without thinking."

"Nah, I reckon you'd have looked at the state of the rucksack and realised. Explains why everything we've found has disintegrated or was bloated like those tins at the supermarket remains. Anyhow, the sun is setting so we'd best be getting off to get the water. Don't know about you but I'm still starving, so we'd best get moving as it won't be many days before we become too weak to fetch any more water."

It took them all of two hours to get back to the stream; lack of food was beginning to take its toll on their bodies, and they had to take frequent stops to rest up.

Both water bottles filled they got back just before sunrise. They could see the moon was three quarters full now, heading towards its last quarter phase and so not providing as much light as when it was closer to being full.

They slumped to the floor of their old apartment and promptly fell asleep.

#

They awoke sometime in the early afternoon and as they ventured out onto the hot patio Robyn suddenly had a thought.

"What with all that's happened, we forgot why we came here. The cellar being used as a pantry!"

"Oh my god, it's under the main house, so might have had some protection." They looked at each other then set off up the connecting path to what had been Judith's home.

Scott looked about as they entered the remains of the building. The roof had caved in here and there exposing the rooms to the full brunt of the bad weather. Signs of the acid rain having its long-term effect showed with the remains of the furniture and wall cupboards collapsed on the floor and ready to disintegrate at a moment's notice.

They carefully made their way through the debris until they reached the hallway just off the kitchen and there was the door. Closed and still intact, that raised their hopes.

Until they found it locked.

Scott was about to barge the door when Robyn demonstrated an aspect of her personality Scott had never seen before when she drop kicked the door in and it shattered, falling down and into the cellar.

Gingerly they made their way down turning on the wind-up torch to light the way. Both let out a sudden shout and they stopped in their tracks staring in horror at the mummified body of Judith.

Robyn shone the torch around examining the scene as she recovered her wits.

"There, her leg is broken. She must have come down here and tripped, broken her leg and not been able to get back up to get out. The stairs would have been almost impossible with a break like that.

Poor woman, she was lovely and kind to us when we arrived."

"I'm guessing that being down here, protected her from whatever happened back then, plus the acid rain and the storms didn't penetrate, so this room was dry which is why she's almost mummified. My heart goes out to her, dying alone down here." Scott added with sadness in his voice.

They squeezed past Judith's remains and carefully pushed the bottom door open to reveal the cellar converted into a storage pantry.

Boxed food duly disintegrated as they touched them showing they had not been spared and the tinned items all bulged suggesting their contents were spoiled.

Dispirited, Robyn and Scott headed back up the stairs and out of the building to return to their own limited accommodation only to realise it was dark and cloudy with drops of painful acid rain falling. Ducking back into Judith's ruined home they headed back to the cellar and sat at the top of the stairs amidst the wreckage of the door they had just destroyed.

There was little to do or say but wait it out until

the storm passed.

#

Almost thirty-six hours passed with loud thunder and terrifying flashes of lightning that startled them with the ferocity of the passing storms.

There was little conversation. Both were by now getting extremely hungry and until the storm abated they couldn't risk trying to get to their room to get the water bottles.

A few hours later, Robyn stirred and realised that apart from Scott's intermittent snoring, everything else was quiet.

The storm fronts had finally passed.

She slid herself away from Scott as he sat slumped against the wall. Taking the torch but waiting until she was back up and out in the hallway she turned it on to find her way out. Stepping outside, Robyn looked up at the sky full of pinpricks of stars with the Milky Way stretching from horizon to horizon and she sighed as she switched the light out.

It was so beautiful, yet now seemed so irrelevant considering they had nothing to eat.

A noise from behind startled her but Scott stepped out and yawned as his stomach rumbled loudly.

"Sorry about that. Can't help it and I don't know what we can do," he offered in a quiet voice.

"I know. Best get to our room with the rucksacks and hope they were protected."

Flicking the torch back on, a few moments later they were relieved to see the rucksacks still dry and well protected, so they grabbed the water bottles and drank deep draughts until satiated.

Scott looked deep in thought as the light from the torch began to fade and he quickly wound it up.

"You know, I think one thing we should do out of respect, is to bury Judith, Danny and Katrina."

"I'd been wondering that too," said Robyn. "I think the sky is beginning to lighten so later in the morning we ought to have a look around to see if there is a shovel or such like still surviving that we can use.

Otherwise, it'll be like those other two skeletons we buried over at the cave hillside, the two women. Pile the stones on top of them."

Looking about they noted one other apartment and headed for it. Another shock awaited them when, as they looked around the top apartment, they discovered the remains of another family of two adults and a child. Their skeletons lay in the main bedroom, huddled together in a desperate act of survival that had not succeeded.

Carefully they collected the remains, took them down to the edge of the property boundary and along with Danny, Trina and Judith's bodies, they buried the group placing as many large stones as possible on each grave to complete the cairns.

Late afternoon, tired and thirsty, not to

mention terribly hungry, Robyn and Scott headed back up to their apartment and drank one of the bottles of water; collapsed into a heap next to each other and fell asleep, exhausted, physically and emotionally.

#

Several days passed and the hunger pangs grew as they stayed in their apartment apart from the occasional trip to replenish the water supply.

After a fitful night's sleep, Robyn came awake to find Scott missing, then she heard it.

Someone, without doubt Scott, was being violently sick somewhere nearby. She raced outside and looked around homing in on the sound and hurried along to what had been Judith's own home, to the place where the pantry was.

Scott was lying on his side clutching his stomach as he again convulsed and threw up. Robyn hurried over then spotted the culprit.

"Oh, you stupid man!" she muttered as she spied the remains of the contents of a once bulging can of whatever it was that Scott had clearly tried to eat. The remains in the tin looked disgusting and she raced back to their room and returned with both water bottles.

Scott downed one in only a couple of gulps, before spewing his guts out again. She held back on the second bottle knowing otherwise she'd have to go back down to the stream, but Scott seemed to settle and wiped his mouth of the vomit and water.

"I know. Don't have to say anything and I'm sorry but I was so hungry I had to try one of them!" Scott stuttered as Robyn relented and handed him the other bottle of water.

Thinking quickly, he poured a little amount into the bottle he'd already used then sipped at that as he handed the nearly full bottle back to Robyn.

"No point spoiling it for you." he said, and she couldn't help but think that he had enough sense to be considerate, even at this stage.

"Thank you. Oh, you are an oaf! How are you feeling?"

"Sore throat and stomach. I won't be trying that again and I can't recommend it!" he said sitting up and taking a deep breath before having a short coughing fit.

"Looks like another trip to the stream for me then. You're in no fit state." Robyn noted as she looked at the empty bottle but offered him the almost full one which he took gratefully.

They headed back to their room, and she made sure he was settled then took both bottles, grabbed her rucksack and spent the next few hours away fetching the water. However, she couldn't help but think she had also begun to wonder about trying the tins down in the pantry.

She was glad she hadn't.

On returning she found Scott fast asleep but

clearly having a nightmare, probably about the tinned food getting its revenge on him for daring to open it up, she mused.

But she was tired from the long walk, and she settled down next to him and promptly fell asleep.

As the days passed, the agony of having no food taunted them as Scott became delirious. Robyn noted he had a fever, but she too was so weak she realised now that it was the end game.

As far as she knew, they were the only ones alive, but she couldn't help wondering if she'd have preferred to have been outside when whatever apocalypse it was had occurred all that time ago. She didn't even know how long it had been, but clearly centuries, possibly even millennia had passed as she slowly sank into a fitful haze and gradually the light of her life force seemed to dim and go out ...

INTERLUDE

EARTH: 12,000 BC
(Before Catastrophe)

The following is translated from from High Alteran for ease of the reader's pleasure and understanding.

They boarded their ship and set off climbing higher towards orbit with the eventual aim of setting off for home world, now their mission was complete. One turned to the other looking somewhat puzzled and indeed a little alarmed.

"Have we missed a stop?" she asked.

Pilot and temporary ship's captain, Sqip looked at the manifest and checked the logs as they continued their ascent away from the northern large continent.

"No, all sites have been logged, why?"

"I have found another case with four hundred still in it."

"WHAT!"

"I have fou ..."

"I heard you, I'm shocked! How? Everything is accounted for."

"I seem to recall that when we left homestation Zalco you mentioned we seemed to be a little over mass, but so little that we both assumed it was a slight mistake in our energy capacity tanks. Perhaps this now explains it as I have run a simulation and indeed the additional mass correlates with the accidental addition of 400 extra units."

"So, it is not *our* fault then?"

"No. What shall we do with them?"

We can't take them back. Let me do another scan, I'll swing low over that peninsular we've just passed over and see if there is anywhere we can place them so they can't be discovered accidentally."

The ship changed course and began to descend, scanning the terrain below it to ascertain possible suitable sites.

"There, right at the end just before the coast, there's a small cave system. We'll put them there." With that Sqip brought the ship down near the top of the hill but noted signs of primitive local humanoid habitation closer to the coast.

"Carf, we had better be careful as there may be local hominids, we'd best avoid them if possible."

"Yes captain. I have the container here so shall we disembark?"

Sqip tilted his head to indicate yes, and they opened the hatch.

The atmosphere on this world was not quite the same as theirs but was just about breathable. Especially after all the exposure they'd had in the last several time periods allocated for achieving their mission goal.

They used their sensor to locate the entrance to the cave which was on one side of the hill they had landed on and around a few decats *(mistranslated - read 'metres')* lower down the hillside. They were

Alterans and tall compared with the incumbent hominids so had to bend down more than they would have liked, as they crawled into the cave.

"You didn't choose wisely!" Carf said a little more sarcastically than she intended.

"I can't believe that's the first time you have complained during this entire mission," proffered Sqip, equally sarcastically. He wasn't very keen on his companion for this mission but had needed to put up with her comments whilst they had a job to do. He'd ask for a transfer if they asked him to work with Carf again!

They crawled in and, using his locator sensor, he spotted two small openings leading into the cave network. Well, at least the larger one did, the smaller led to a dead end. They chose to go for the deeper system.

They found a spot and marvelled at the fresh markings on the walls depicting local hunters and their quarry. Impressive considering how deep they were and how dark and almost inaccessible it was. On a hunch Sqip indicated for them to turn off their lights and for a moment they were plunged into darkness.

Only for a moment for there seemed to be a faint source of light further down so Sqip continued deeper into the cave system, curiosity rising. Carf followed but left the case behind just in case they ran into trouble. The ship could be operated remotely, and she could tell from her arm controls that its signal easily penetrated through the rock from above so she was confident that if anything untoward happened, they could get out if needed.

The light ahead seemed to flicker but gave enough luminance for their sensitive eyes to see the tunnel, until suddenly, ahead of them there stood a terrified humanoid, naked but completely covered in thick brown matted hair. He saw them, panicked with a terrified look about his face and fled, heading deeper into the system.

Sqip realised they had to mind wipe him otherwise there was a chance it could affect the future development of this unusual species with intelligence potential.

The humanoid reached a section that had columnar like solidified vertical lava and seemed to know his way as he edged along the columns holding his flaming torch to light the way.

He turned only to see the strange beings appear behind and look straight at him. He was distracted and shocked enough by their frightening appearance to miss his step, slip and plunge down to a ledge below, cracking open his skull and bleeding to death. His last views were of strange beings that he could not comprehend. His torch lay still clutched in his hand as the last wisps of life ebbed away.

The torch flickered out.

Sqip looked at Carf and did another tilt of his head.

"Scans show no life signs. Looks like I won't

need to mind wipe him after all. Poor thing. Was scared out of its tiny little mind."

Carf looked dispassionately at Sqip.

"Let us hope that wasn't an important humanoid for the future development of this planet!"

"We'll never know now, that is certain." Sqip replied as that was also on his mind, but the deed was done so he indicated for them to head back upwards to the wider cave they had found. There was no need for them to report this little incident, no reason to get themselves into unnecessary trouble back home.

Once back where they had left the case, they set about placing the small crystals around the cave walls where over time they would grow, but found they still had some left over.

Continuing back up towards the entrance they placed the remaining crystals in the dead-end cave nearer the surface, not ideal but there was no way they were taking them back with them on the journey home. They reached its tight entrance, exited and took out their sidearms.

In two short bursts of their small-scale weapons the upper entrance was sealed with rock debris covering and hiding the entrance and then using the scanners the lower entrance, much tighter was also sealed to prevent any of the hominids accidentally discovering the, now unusual, caves before they were sufficiently advanced.

Finally, reaching orbit was a great relief. They prepared to set off for homeworld as Sqip checked their instructions on completion of their primary mission.

"Well, that's it. According to the GAA's best minds, if the humanoids do develop intelligence then they will either figure out their star will have a bad phase in twelve thousand of their orbits and they will expand out into their solar system to ensure their survival."

"And if they don't develop enough in time?"

"Hopefully some will discover the sites we've set up and be protected. Although the last one we have just done is highly unlikely as it wasn't on the projected possible sites of regular humanoid development. It doesn't matter anyway to us as we will be long gone by then."

"When is this catastrophic event expected to occur did you say?"

"I just said, was you not being attentive? They can't be that exact, but in about twelve thousand of their orbits of their star."

"Is that really enough time to develop into a sophisticated civilisation? Seems a bit short to me!"

"No idea, I don't care personally either as I think it is a waste of time but someone much higher than us thinks it is important, so we've done our bit. Let's go home."

"That's the best thing you have said since we arrived here at this awful planet." Carf bent over and kissed her lifelong companion as he smiled. Setting course for Alteran, Sqip knew that in the end, he'd never really want to swap her for another and if truth were told he did prefer working with his life partner than some other unknown Alteran!

They left the odd solar system that had caught the GAA's attention, never to know what would become of the hominids and how they would develop from such a primitive state.

Or even if any of those said hominids would discover the caves and be protected when the predicted cataclysm was due to take place…

DISCOVERY

CHAPTER 16: WHAT? WHERE? HOW?

She stirred and every part of her body screamed out in pain as she tried to move. Her eyes were stinging and for a few moments all she could see was a diffuse glow through her eyelids.

Robyn tried to take a deep breath, but her chest screamed out in pain and someone came to her side, a dull formless shape. She felt a rising panic as the form seemed ...*alien.*

She was desperate to scream but couldn't, then something happened to her arm, a slight very quick pinprick and she lost consciousness again.

#

Groggy.

Was she dead or alive?

If alive, why did it feel like she'd be better off dead? Her hearing was almost non-existent and although there were faint muffled sounds, she couldn't move her head to see where they came from. She drifted back into unconsciousness again.

#

The lights, they were so bright even through her eyelids. She tried to open her mouth, but something was lodged in her throat and she realised she couldn't speak anyway. A feeling of dread, tinged with some relief coursed through her conscious mind.

She should be dead.

They were the only ones left.

Perhaps not.

Was this heaven?

By the amount of pain, probably hell!

Where was Scott?

She drifted off into slumberland as her brain became overtired again.

#

Sounds.

Muffled but a little clearer than before.

Words!

It sounded like words, but she couldn't make out what was being said. There was some sensation of light, but her eyelids were still stuck tight. But they were able to move!

The eyelids weren't stuck together, there was something covering her face instead.

The pain.

It was almost gone, and she felt a warmth throughout her body, soothing, healing perhaps?

Sensation of movement around her with changing shades of light filtering through the covering then she felt something touch the side of her head.

Someone was taking off the bandages and as the light increased she found herself shutting her eyelids tightly and found the light blindingly bright.

Her hearing was coming back as she heard someone say something and the lights seemed to dim. The bandage came fully off, and she squinted but still felt her neck and head were sore. She couldn't turn her body, but someone seemed to bend over her and do something.

The drops in her eyes stung briefly but then she relaxed as they began to soothe her eyes and she found she could open them up.

People!

Not aliens after all!

A sense of elation swept through her, yet she still couldn't move but did try to smile. Then wondered if they were friendly. They had to be. For heaven's sake, they were looking after her. She tried to sit up but as the people gathered round and held her gently, she passed out from the effort.

#

Robyn stirred and groggily opened her eyes as she instinctively moved her arms to push herself up into a sitting position. Someone helped her and as the haze cleared from her eyes the woman came into view clear and sharp.

Oriental. Quite strikingly pretty yet in a strong, powerful sort of way.

"That better for you?" the stranger asked, and her voice was the exact opposite of what Robyn had expected, smooth, gentle and with a sense of control of the situation. It also sounded a little stilted too.

Robyn opened her mouth but for a few moments she couldn't speak until the woman gently inserted a tube into her mouth and a warm soothing liquid flowed into her as her throat welcomed the sensation.

She swallowed several times and held her throat for a few moments, carefully rubbing it.

"Yes, that's much better now, thank you."

The woman smiled and nodded as another hove into view and looked inquisitively at her colleague. Caucasian.

"Progress at last then?" she asked of the first woman.

"Yes, it would appear so."

Robyn watched, fascinated as their lips didn't seem to match what she was hearing, and she tried to raise her right hand to get their attention.

The first woman looked at her.

"How do you feel now you are out of the worst?"

"I'm not sure.

Where am I?

Where is Scott?

I need to see him. Where is he?" Panic began to rise in Robyn's chest as she looked about the room but there was only her bed in it and no sign of Scott.

The second woman gently held her left hand.

"Ahh, your companion. He is not quite as far along as you are, but we think he will make a full recovery. We have to look after you both for now and when he is improved I am sure you will be allowed to see and meet up."

That only partially reassured her, but Robyn knew she was not strong enough yet to stand so had to take their word for it.

"Where am I?"

"In the medical care centre of Theta." came the reply, but naturally it didn't mean anything to Robyn.

"No, I mean, what country? England, or still in Portugal?"

The two women looked at each other and shook their heads.

"So, somewhere else then? America, Australia, must be somewhere that speaks English…"

The nearer of the two shook her head and looked puzzled.

"We don't understand any of those names. Where have you been and why were you in the restricted zone?"

"I, I don't understand."

"One of our teams spotted signs of unusual disturbance in a barren area of the restricted zone. We don't understand how you could have got there or where you are from," said the oriental one.

"Or even survived there. Although, it was touch and go and we did find remains of two others along with several very old skeletal remains," added the Caucasian woman.

Robyn felt faint as she tried to understand what they were getting at and tried to shake her head but slumped back into unconsciousness.

The closer of the two women turned to her companion.

"I did say it was too early for us to begin the questions."

"Yes, you were correct. However, I did recognise a few of the names she mentioned. They are from the Sagas."

"No!"

"Yes. Either this is an elaborate hoax or…"

"They are both from the pre-era?"

"Precisely."

They looked at each other stunned yet knew they needed more information before informing their superiors.

CHAPTER 17: THE MEETING

They both sat quietly in the small yet adequately furnished accommodation they had been assigned. However, nether Robyn nor Scott had been given any answers as to where they were, or how long they had been 'away for'.

Scott had recovered only to learn from Robyn that their 'helpers' seemed also to be their prison guards. She had been effectively kept in the dark with none of her questions being answered, but an apparent disbelief when she had mentioned countries that the two nurses, or whatever they were, seemed to be unaware of.

There was a window and they looked out over a wonderful view of rolling waves and a long sandy beach with rocky outcrops in the distance. It seemed familiar yet strange as not once had either of them seen any signs of life such as birds or literally any form of insect life as they looked out.

"We're prisoners, aren't we?" Robyn voiced her fears as Scott looked out of the window.

He turned to her and shrugged. "We're alive, we've been rescued and brought back to health, have been fed and clothed. But yes, it does seem like it, doesn't it!"

"I don't know which is worst, surviving, or knowing that everything and everyone we once knew is no longer alive," she replied despondently as Scott cuddled her to give her some moral support.

The door slid open and the one they now knew as Shalita entered with a tray of food and drinks. She was possibly far eastern, Philippine, with a golden skin tone that was beautiful to see.

"How are we today?" she asked as Robyn and Scott eyed her warily. Shalita set the tray down on the raised central platform that served as a table and smiled at them.

"You both look very healthy now. Not like when you were first brought to us. If it helps, I have been asked to inform you that you are very special people and as such are to be treated with the very best of our abilities."

Scott looked at her and did wonder if they were being a little too cautious and reserved. Robyn spoke before he had a chance to say anything.

"Thank you Shalita. I am sure Scott will agree that we do appreciate that you have cared for us and brought us back from close to death. But we just want some answers, and nobody is telling us what we want, no, I mean, *need* to know."

"Then I have good news for you. You have three visitors and if I understand correctly, they have been instructed to answer as best they can. Oh, here they are now."

The door had slid open again but only two people came through, both the medical staff that had been looking after them whilst they recovered.

Shalita looked and smiled at the pair, and they smiled back at her, indicating she could stay. The slightly taller oriental woman stood looking out of the window as her companion walked up to Robyn and Scott and shook them warmly by the hand.

"It is so very good to see how well you have both recovered. You gave us quite a task, especially you, Scott. My name is Carmalie and my colleague is Dasheeda." On hearing her name Dasheeda came over to them and also shook their hands, then both sat opposite the couple.

Dasheeda now spoke in a slightly lower, deeper voice.

"We know only too well that you have been through a very traumatic time and if we are to be open and honest with you, you are both a puzzle and a miracle as far as we are concerned." She looked at Carmalie to continue.

"You ask regularly what year it is. This is difficult for us to answer as you mention that it was 2037 AD and it was something called a month, I believe you said, July?"

"Yes, that's right." offered Scott. Robyn nodded.

"We were on holiday in the Algarve when something disastrous happened to the world."

"But how did you come to survive it?" asked Dasheeda quietly.

"We don't know, but we were exploring a small cave system near where our holiday villa was situated when there was several earth tremors, and we became trapped deep inside the cave system." Robyn looked at Scott for confirmation and he nodded agreement and took up the story.

"We tried to get out via the way we entered but a rock fall had cut us off, so we headed back down the only route we knew but for some reason we fell asleep," he said.

Robyn shuffled in her seat. "The crystals. They were glowing all around us as we seemed to pass out. The next thin…"

"Crystals?" asked Carmalie with a puzzled look about her. Robyn continued.

"Yes, it was very odd but there were crystals, lots of them in and located all through the largest part of the cave; they were all glowing an eerie purplish colour. That was the last thing I remember before waking and finding we were caked in a layer of dust, and we couldn't open our eyes or mouths."

"Our torches were drained but luckily we had a wind-up torch and the water bottles we had, helped clear our eyes and mouths so we could breathe easier. It was quite frightening," added Scott.

"The Algarve. Is that where our scout found you?" asked Carmalie, fascinated.

"Err, yes, once we managed to find a way out of the cave system, everywhere above ground was desolate. No vegetation or any form of life when we began to explore to find food and water. We found buildings destroyed, vehicles eroded to almost nothing and skeletons. We had to accept that we had wiped ourselves out."

Shalita looked at them oddly, she'd been quiet and was not as experienced as her two colleagues, but she was puzzled by this revelation.

"I do not understand how you can be wiped out, yet you are here?"

Both Robyn and Scott chuckled and shook their heads.

"A figure of speech, I mean the various countries of the world. Some were on one side and others against them in their beliefs. Several times they had come close to destroying each other and the rest of us once they had weapons such as nuclear bombs and the ability to launch them into space," offered Scott.

Robyn was herself puzzled by something. "You seem not to know about countries or familiar places such as the Algarve. It's odd as your ancestors must have survived for you all to be here."

"I fear that the earth has changed far more than you could have imagined," said Dasheeda quietly. "You see there are no longer these things you call countries. Our broken history records suggests there were lots of groups across the world and some didn't get along with the others, perhaps these are the 'countries' you speak of?"

Robyn nodded but was a little bewildered.

"So, what country are we in then exactly? Does the name the United Kingdom or Great Britain mean anything?"

All three shook their heads.

"America? Europe? China? Russia?" Scott added.

Again, Shalita, Carmalie and Dasheeda shook their heads.

"So where on earth are we then and I'm guessing the name won't mean anything to us will it?"

The three looked at each other and Carmalie tilted her head a little then stood up and walked over to the window.

Scott had been studying the view and spoke up in anticipation.

"That looks like close to where we were staying, it is very like the coastline of the Algarve which was in a country known as Portugal."

Carmalie seemed to have a wry smile about her as she looked at the view.

"I think it is time we replaced this."

She did something with a small almost bandage like strap on her wrist and the view suddenly changed.

Robyn and Scott stared in utter disbelief and shock.

A two thirds illuminated *Earth* hung in a jet-black star filled sky halfway up the view and spread out before them was a desolate landscape, illuminated by harsh light. Extensive domes and buildings extended out in various directions almost filling what Scott took to be a huge crater.

"You are not on the *Earth*, but on the *Moon*..."

and Carmalie saw both their charges faint with the shock of the revelation.

CHAPTER 18: EXPLANATIONS

It was a day later, or at least that's what it felt like to the couple, after they had recovered from their shock.

They barely spoke, such was the weight of the knowledge that incredibly they were not on Earth at all but on the Moon.

"Must be artificial gravity. But the view was so lifelike, and you could see round at an angle on all sides, so it really did look like a window looking out at the sea," muttered Scott just loud enough for Robyn to hear. She kept staring at the lunar landscape and shaking her head.

"But the view doesn't seem to change, the Earth is still in the same place. Wouldn't it have moved or something if the moon is turning?" she asked out loud, but not particularly in Scott's direction.

"I don't think so. Danny once told me about it. Something to do with the moon keeping the same side facing the earth so we see the moon go around us but from any one part of the side of the moon facing the Earth, it would stay where it was but slowly change its phase." Scott was impressed by how much he had remembered from his long-deceased friend.

"Ahh, yes, now I see what was tormenting me. Now I look at the Earth and it's not quite lit up like the other day. Scott, I feel overwhelmed. Life on

Earth almost wiped out, no idea how long we were, I don't know what to call it... frozen in place? Yes, sort of frozen in place and time ...

... and we're on the moon dammit!"

"On the moon ... There were only two bases set up, the China/Russia base and the so called 'international' base set up by the US, Europe, us and a few others, I can't remember who they were. But what can be seen out there is more than a city scale base."

"LOOK!" shouted Robyn and Scott joined her as he followed her right arm and finger pointing to something slowly rising in the distance. A spaceship of some kind but with nothing that could be used to tell its scale, it could have been a few feet across or several miles ...

It soared off in the opposite direction to them, so they didn't get a better look, but it did seem to show the view was a real live one. It was also headed toward the Earth.

"I'm still not convinced we had technology that could create a view like this. Just think of the movies of the time. Even old-fashioned CGI didn't look a patch on what was done with that time travel saga - 'Time Stretch' I think it was called." Scott knew he was probably wrong.

"Danny took me to see that, but it was rubbish, poor acting but yeah, the effects were pretty neat.

I do hope it's not simulated after the shock of seeing the Earth up there like that."

"I see now what you meant earlier. Yes, there

is more night-time on the Earth from our view so we're losing the daytime side of it.

What bit I can make out looks browner than I think it should be and I reckon that's Oz at lower left so we're probably looking at the Pacific at night."

"Hah! Well, if that bit down there is Australia then it was normally red, orange and brown anyway as climate change was rendering it almost impossible to live there." Robyn seemed satisfied with her observation, but it still made her feel hollow.

"They're all gone..."

"Yes."

"Everyone we knew..."

Scott didn't reply this time as he could tell they were both becoming despondent at their plight.

Almost on cue there was a chiming sound and after a short pause the door slid open to reveal the three people from the previous day entering.

"Good day to you both, do you feel well enough to continue?" Carmalie looked at them in turn, smiling disarmingly.

Robyn looked at Scott and shrugged.

"Well, not like we can go anywhere else is there!"

"That depends. Once we understand what happened to you and how we can fit it with what we know, then we will be able to take you on a tour of Theta." Dasheeda chimed in, still with that low, quiet, but relaxing deep voice.

"What about going back to Earth?" suggested Scott not really knowing what he'd expect to find there but it is, was, home.

"At some point if you wish," came the surprising answer from Carmalie and Scott and Robyn looked at each other and back at the three a little stunned.

"I, I thought it was bad down there?" asked Robyn cautiously.

"Yes, it is true that large areas have yet to recover, and our long-term strategy is beginning to show results so at the moment there are a few places that are habitable without any protection required."

Shalita now joined in the conversation. "Where you were discovered is still in the early stages of recovery, but we have four hundred sites that are habitable, although most are underground." she added.

"Shall we continue?" hinted Carmalie as she indicated to the soft seats where they'd all sat the previous day.

Settling down, Robyn was still inquisitive.

"So, one question you didn't answer was how long we had been, how do I put this, asleep. Preserved? Whatever..."

"We have been pondering that very question and we have a surprising result that confirms our suspicions when you first awoke and started talking about countries and places that were not familiar to us. You see we don't have a complete historical record because so much was destroyed in the disaster." Carmalie was about to continue but Scott now joined in.

"Hold on, I've noticed something that should have been more apparent. Your lips move but what I, and I guess Robyn, hears isn't quite the same. How is that?"

Dasheeda smiled and looked at her companions.

"Very good observation, we had hoped that it was so natural that you wouldn't notice but it is good that you have. It shows a good intellect. Let us say we have special implants that intercept the sound waves before the ear actually hears them.

A small organic device has been implanted in us from birth and now you yourselves as soon as you were well enough to cope with the minor but delicate operation. It allows us to understand each other without the barrier of different languages getting in the way."

Shalita continued. "Our language has evolved from what we think was called Angliscise and interestingly you both speak something very similar."

"Ahh, it's called English, after our mother country's main language," smiled Scott but Robyn looked at him in a funny way that the other three couldn't interpret.

"Excuse me dear sir, but you're forgetting I'm part Welsh!"

Scott chuckled, then looked at Carmalie.

"It's complicated! But nonetheless the main language was known as English. It was considered the main language of most of the world, but didn't stop other countries using their own languages in their own countries."

Carmalie looked thoughtful then spoke. "So, what we can confirm is that in the distant past the world was fractured into many different thinking groups of humans. And these groups were these 'countries' you speak of. At some point in the near future, it would be helpful if you could give us as much detail about how many of them and where they were located as I believe some of our data has been misinterpreted."

It was Robyn that picked up on something Carmalie had said.

"Distant past? I asked about how long we had been sort of asleep or preserved for…?"

Dasheeda looked at Carmalie who nodded and Dasheeda spoke.

"Our fractured records suggest that the disaster occurred three thousand three hundred and eighty-four years ago…"

Stunned silence as Robyn and Scott absorbed the news.

Carmalie saw the look of anguish in their eyes.

"In many ways, you are the lucky ones. I have to ask a delicate question as it is directly related to you both. Do you feel able to carry on at the moment?"

Scott took a deep breath and looked at Robyn

who nodded agreement.

"I guess that's a yes. It is no good prolonging our agony. Ask away."

"You will understand the only reason we knew about you were the burials you made. They were changes that were picked up by our monitoring satellites and alerted us to something that did not appear to be a natural occurrence. One of our teams was dispatched to investigate."

Robyn looked sadly down then seemed to gather her strength.

"We were two couples on holiday, we all went for a walk because our local holiday villa owner had recommended we do some walking and explore a cave system not far from the villa.

The other couple liked to sit out in the sun and relax but we enjoyed exploration, so ventured into the cave. That's when the disaster took place trapping us inside. What we didn't know at the time was the other couple, Danny and Katrina had rushed into the upper section of the cave to escape the devastation. They too seemed to be preserved but being closer to the surface were exposed to the radiation from what we assume were the blasts and fallout from a nuclear war."

Scott took up the story.

"We discovered they had made their way back to the site of our holiday villa, but they were extremely ill and died as we tried to comfort them. We also found the skeletal remains of several others staying at the villa complex, plus Judith the owner. They must have died in the devastation caused by the war, so we felt we had to give them a decent burial."

"I see. A matter for clarification, but there was no war. It was a natural catastrophe. The sun experienced a series of what we think was unprecedented violent bouts of activity that threw out a continuous series of solar flares of the highest magnitude, several of which bombarded the Earth over several days. The ozone layer was severely depleted, and we estimate that around ten percent of the oceans boiled away, surface life was extinguished including several hundreds of metres down from the surface."

Robyn turned to Scott.

"Danny said something was odd about the sky, but you just laughed it off as his not being used to the clear blue sky of the Algarve. But he was into astronomy, and he really did spot something was wrong."

"I guess so, but think of it this way. If we'd been spooked about it and headed back to the villa we probably would have died like everyone else on Earth."

Robyn sat taking that in.

"Good point, I guess so," she said slowly. "It still all feels unreal to me, as if I'm going to wake up from a bad dream."

Scott gently put his arm around her, and they just looked into each other's eyes. Shalita saw this.

"It is clear you are both, I believe they called

it 'an item', and this must be an impossible circumstance for you to come to terms with. Perhaps it would be best if we continue this later today. I have arranged for your lunch to be brought in here in a short while." She looked at her companions who nodded in agreement and stood before leaving the couple to absorb and ponder on what they had been told.

CHAPTER 19: THEIR SIDE OF THE STORY

Incredibly, instead of the three women coming to them, for the first time Robyn and Scott were amazed to see a man at the door when it chimed, the first time they had seen a male since their remarkable rescue and recovery.

"Shalita has asked if you would like to accompany me to the meeting in another location which may help with arrangements."

He was quite tall with fair hair and a slightly golden complexion. Under different circumstances Robyn would have happily gone on a date with him, in another distant time and place of course.

Scott wasn't quite as impressed but knew there wasn't really a choice. He didn't have a chance to say anything as Robyn just smiled at the newcomer and indicated they would follow him.

"So, what do they call you?" she asked innocently.

"Paolo."

It was a short and simple answer.

"Hello Paolo, my name is Robyn, and this is Scott," she replied as she smiled up at him.

"Hello to you both. Now, if you come along and step on this travelator it won't be long before we reach our destination.

Scott noted that Paolo didn't respond to the

flirtatious overture that Robyn seemed to be trying to convey in her softly spoken words. He, however, was more interested in the travelator, which reminded him of the escalators of their own time, but far more advanced.

"Step onto it and once we are on, it will begin motion," said Paolo and they did as he asked. It began to move, slowly, then a little faster but not so much as to cause disorientation. At first they seemed to travel down a long corridor built with clear walls, so they were able to watch the equivalent of buildings pass by and in the distance, the dome that protected them from the harshness of space, but then they approached and entered a tunnel.

It was evenly illuminated with no flickering lights which felt odd as there were no reference points to indicate they were actually moving, except for the faint impression of speed they had from the vibrations of the floor and a slight breeze in their faces.

Ahead, in the distance, a light blue section of the tunnel appeared and steadily grew larger. They entered it, slowing down until they emerged out of the tunnel into a large expanse that could have been mistaken for a huge outdoor area with trees, a large variety of flowering plants of a multitude of sizes and shapes, along with areas set aside with seating accommodation.

Overhead and almost too distant to see, the domed roof just showed a faint smattering of stars but otherwise it almost appeared like a normal daytime scene, albeit on the Moon.

Except that the Earth was just visible lower down off to their right, just to remind them it seemed, of where they really were.

They stopped and Paolo stepped off indicating the three people in the distance sitting awaiting their arrival.

All the while, one thing kept bothering Scott. *Where were the rest of the people?*

They approached Carmalie, Dasheeda and Shalita who all stood and smiled at them as Shalita indicated for them all to sit.

Scott had to break his silence and say something before they had a chance to start, what he still kept feeling was their interrogation.

"Where is everyone?"

Shalita actually laughed a little and shook her head.

"I'm sorry, it had not occurred to us to explain about Theta. It is still being constructed, most of it is operational but yet to be populated. Theta is I believe from an ancient language, 'eek' which amuses some of our populace and it is the eighth such establishment on the Moon."

Robyn in turn now laughed.

"You really do need us to fill in lots of gaps. It is not 'eek' but Greek, from the country of Greece in southeastern Europe. You are using the Greek alphabet which itself is the first two letters of their *alphabet*, Alpha and Beta."

"Yes, well I guess you could say that it is all Greek to me" chuckled Scott as Robyn shook her head slowly at him and smiled.

The other four sat looking bemused and perplexed at them so Scott knew he had to elaborate.

"It's an old joke from our time so I guess it doesn't really work here now. Sorry."

"On the contrary, we do have lots we can learn from you both, as the others never recovered," replied Carmalie but Scott and Robyn stopped chuckling and looked at the foursome in shock.

"Others?" they both said in unison, stunned.

"Please, there is a lot for us to tell you, so this is why we wanted a better location, much more pleasant for you both." Dasheeda quickly added. "You see you are the fifteenth to suddenly appear out of nowhere and to have been in some form of hibernation since the disaster or calamity that befell the Earth.

You two are the first to have survived seemingly intact and unscathed. The others sadly appear to have been subjected to much too high a dose of radiation, even though our impression was that they too were deep underground. Most of them also mentioned glowing crystals so naturally that seems to be the key, but we have never found any that are what you can call active."

Carmalie took up the narrative. "A team explored the area where you were found and indeed discovered the cave system. They found signs that you were nearly two hundred metres deep, far deeper than any of the others including the two companions you said were in the upper part of the cavern.

The crystals found appear at first sight to be simply quartz, but we suspect there is something more to them than that. There were also far more crystal formations than we'd expect in that sort of geology. This is why it is a puzzle."

"We have no idea how, why or who placed them there as they are not natural," added Shalita. "So far you two are the luckiest humans of all to have survived like this."

Scott was himself puzzled however as clearly other humans must have survived.

"But I don't understand. How did your ancestors survive then, if they weren't in caves deep underground when the ozone layer was destroyed? It doesn't make sense."

"And this is why we are here now, for us to explain our side of what happened and why you see all of this around us," said Carmalie.

She drew a deep breath.

"You would quite rightly think that with all life extinguished on the surface and extending down many metres that nothing could survive.

However, around the planet, there were a large number of very deep underground establishments that had been designed and built to be fully independent in case of either a natural disaster or global war. We are aware that nuclear weapons had been amassed and that despite a brief respite for a few decades, the world apparently had turned hostile again," explained Carmalie.

"Tell us about it, the number of times we thought the US and the western world were going to get into conflict with Russia and China seemed to be at least twice a year. The last time for us when they almost came to blows was just as both sides completed their first moonbases and a Russian cargo craft lost control and crashed just a few miles from the US/International base," said Robyn, remembering how scared she had been watching the newscasts come in.

"At a later time, if you can give us as much information like this as you , it will help fill in our gaps and that would be most appreciated," chimed in Shalita as Carmalie nodded, then continued.

"There were around fifty deep sea bases too, along with a variety of submarines that stayed submerged, many for over a year. Those that surfaced too soon found the radiation levels too high and suffered consequently.

But although everything in orbit had also been destroyed, these deep underground facilities eventually established communications with the undersea establishments and slowly they came together to work for survival.

Everything surface wise was destroyed beyond redemption and a large number of the surviving establishments had not been designed to hold the whole world's records, hence our own records of the history before the calamity is patchy.

We believe your talk of 'countries' confirms what some scholars have said for a long time, that part of the human race's downfall was the fact it was broken up into so many different regions, beliefs and languages that it is almost a miracle humans survived , without the natural calamity that struck the Earth."

Dasheeda took up the story. "Those bases scattered around the world and undersea eventually formed our civilisation and having a head start in terms of technology, our species expanded until we could colonise a few small areas on the surface once the radiation had dropped to acceptable levels.

Interestingly, something was slowly replacing the ozone layer and our investigations found that although life down to several hundred meters had been extinguished, primitive life forms much deeper were beginning to thrive and began to produce oxygen, subsequently helping to create a new ozone layer.

Knowing that having just the one planet habitable where almost all life on Earth could be extinguished in such a short period of time, we quickly rediscovered how to get into space and made it a priority. A large area of the Earth is still not fully habitable, as I believe you may have discovered due to the extensive and violent storms that sweep through those regions.

Although there was little in the way of

life where you were discovered, in other places vegetation and insect life is beginning to return. This is partly down to our own efforts over time with various DNA and seed banks that were part of the reason the underground establishments were constructed.

Also, partly due to a deep seated insect population gradually emerging closer to the surface. We expect in time that the earth will regain some aspects of its former glory, but we are still in the early stages."

"Wow, even after three or so thousand years it seems it will take much longer then?" asked Robyn and Carmalie nodded.

"Yes. So for now that is all we can divulge, but if you can help us fill in our historical knowledge for the time being, then we can look at allowing you more freedom once you become acquainted with our way of life.

I should state that our date system is not based on the year of the calamity, but year zero was set when we finally were able to explore the earth's surface which took about a thousand years. So, our calendar starts a thousand years after the calamity and our current year is two thousand, three hundred and eighty-nine years."

"So, you should really say three thousand, three hundred and eighty-nine years for the date if our dating system had been continued?" said Robyn out loud to no one in particular.

"The calendar is what was decided by the

surviving ancestors, so we don't have any more say in the matter and just proceed with what was decreed," added Dasheeda.

Carmalie continued, ignoring Dasheeda. "We will arrange for Paolo to stay with you to help with the equipment and access you will need and in time we in turn will look at integrating you more fully into our society."

Scott winced slightly at the thought that Paolo was going to help them as he carefully stole a look at Robyn who naturally seemed delighted at the news.

Paolo seemed nonplussed by the news as he took them back to their accommodation in silence.

#

Shalita, Carmalie and Dasheeda looked at each other in turn then Shalita swiped for a holoscreen and another figure appeared before them.

"I noted you were trying to contact us. Have you news?"

"Yes, there are two issues, confirmation on both counts," answered the figure.

"Does the first affect the second?" asked Dasheeda.

"Unlikely," came the reply.

"How long on the first?

"Five or possibly six…"

"And the second?"

"Two."

"Thank you for the update. That is all," replied Shalita and the figure vanished as the holoscreen closed down.

She turned to her colleagues, and they just nodded without a word...

CHAPTER 20: REVELATIONS

Scott need not have worried, despite several flirtatious attempts by Robyn over the next few days towards Paolo, he was not interested and generally remained a little aloof to her.

Scott found himself talking more with Paolo who, it transpired, was romantically involved with Shalita. Their hosts had watched with a little bemusement how Robyn had quickly fallen for Paolo, despite his best efforts of not engaging with her romantically.

Robyn was a little crestfallen once Paolo had gently informed her that he was not interested and she struggled for a while to talk to Scott to make up for her folly, he in turn just took it all in his stride.

Paolo taught them how to use the screens that seemed to be like holographic projections and how to conjure them up with the correct hand gestures. It felt a little like magic to Scott and Robyn, but Paolo explained that they were constantly surrounded by a special field that they could access with subtle gestures.

"So, was this field all around us when we first emerged out of the cave when we were on Earth?" asked Scott inquisitively.

"No, when we are anywhere on the surface of a world outside the enclosed establishments we have personal field generators if it is felt they are required. They are not always needed but can be useful to convey complex information quickly to the nearest such establishment."

Scott knew something Paolo had just said seemed to catch his attention and it took a few seconds for him to realise what it was.

"Worlds, you say? You mean Earth and the Moon then?"

Robyn looked at Scott then she realised what could be implied whilst Paolo actually smiled and swiped up for a holo display to appear.

"I have been informed you are ready for more details such as this." He showed the Earth with dozens of locations scattered around the globe showing where humanity was reclaiming the planet. Then he zoomed out to the moon and showed the eight domed establishments. A ninth was marked, but dark compared with the rest and Paolo explained it was only just beginning construction.

He again did something with his hand and the view raced across space to Mars where five domed cities had been established. But it didn't stop there. He swiped again and with virtual reality they sped across space to Jupiter and down to the moon Europa with a solitary base, then quickly up again and off to Saturn. This time to the moon called Enceladus with a base near the south polar region with large fissures that appeared to be active.

But it still didn't stop as they moved outwards

to orbiting facilities at both Uranus and Neptune. The views were breath-taking.

Scott and Robyn's minds were reeling but Paolo changed the view one final time to bring them back inwards to the asteroid belt. He explained what they'd witnessed.

"After the disaster, once our civilisation had settled down to an ordered state and we began to progress once again, it was unanimously agreed that we needed to ensure humanity's survival. By establishing as many colonies as possible or bases in your terms on other suitable worlds was a priority.

We do not desecrate the major worlds for their materials, but now mine the minor worlds that are scattered between Mars and Jupiter along with the icy minor worlds further out. I believe at some stage soon we are to take a voyage out to show them to you as part of your official integration into our civilisation."

"That sounds amazing and so democratic at the same time," offered Robyn as her mind reeled at what she had seen.

"You are for us, unique and so highly valued as new members of our civilisation. It is the least we can do. I have some interesting news for you about a couple of gadgets that we found with you that didn't seem to do anything.

Our scientists were able to carefully take them apart and figured how they worked. Their power sources had failed so they reverse engineered how to power them and connect them to our systems.

However, you will also be pleased to know that Shalita intervened and prevented them from looking at the information that was stored on the devices as she believed, as do the rest of us, that there may be personal information on the devices.

Here you are."

Paolo handed over the smartphones to the astonished pair who grinned like it was their birthdays. Something familiar in an unfamiliar world. It took Scott a few minutes to remember his pass code, but Robyn was immediately scrolling through photos, videos and apps that she thought she would never see again. Paolo smiled as they became engrossed in the devices and quietly left them to it.

The pair quickly realised that most apps needed Internet connectivity and indeed, somewhere that was actually holding the data servers, and, as they were all gone, the apps just crashed. However, those apps designed to work wholly on the smartphones offline continued to operate, except for a few that kept trying to download updates which quickly failed.

The next day Shalita, Carmalie and Dasheeda entered with Paolo. Robyn and Scott were immediately concerned as it had been a while since all four had joined them as a group at the same time.

Dasheeda quickly spoke up seeing their mounting concern. "No worries. We need to share some more information with you to help you adjust to the wider society."

As they took their usual seats, Shalita brought up a holoscreen and quickly showed the solar system starting with the orbit of the earth and moon.

"As Paolo showed you yesterday, we have explored and expanded out into the solar system.

But there is more. You see, once we had stabilised our society and demonstrated we had learned how to look after our worlds, we were *contacted*."

"Sorry, what?" Scott's mind began to race, and he wondered if what Danny had often told him was actually true.

"You may or may not remember right at the beginning that I was going to bring someone else in to meet you shortly after you were well enough to begin to converse. But it was felt to be too soon, so now we feel it is the right time.

She pressed a small patch on her wrist and spoke. "Please enter, we believe they are ready."

The door slid open and in entered a being that made both Robyn and Scott stare for a few moments with their mouths open in shock and surprise.

"May I introduce to you Chel. He is from the planet Alteran. It orbits a star almost forty light years away. As you can see he is quite tall so being here is a little discomforting to him, but he wanted to meet you both."

"Thank you for seeing me and I hope you have recovered enough to ask me any questions." Chel said as the couple just sat stunned in silence.

Chel turned to the others. "Are they well? Am I being translated correctly?"

"Oh, err, sorry Mr Chel, my name is Robyn, and this is Scott." Robyn looked up at Chel's smiling face and couldn't decide if she should be afraid or laugh as he did look a little comical.

"Chel, that is my name, and I am pleased you are well. I have heard a great deal about you both. Shalita has asked me to explain the wider picture to you. The civilisation you humans know as earth and humanity, we know as the Terran civilisation. Humanity is a small part of what is called in your language, the Galactic Arm Association which consists of 297 civilisations, incorporating 416 sentient species who have wholeheartedly taken on board the GAA values and practises.

We all trade peacefully with each other and settle our differences in a civilised way. I have asked that Shalita and Paolo explain more, but I have something to say to you all as this also concerns the Terran society at large.

Your appearance is not totally unforeseen, you see our best scientists, just over fifteen thousand of your orbits ago, were able to predict the natural calamity that befell your fledgling society. It was predicted that your type of central star would undergo a series of internal adjustments as part of the natural process but that would also entail extremely high chances of what you call solar flares of a type that would certainly destroy carbon-based life forms on the planet.

At that time the human cultures were observed as being quite primitive yet holding much promise. In order to give them a chance, tens of thousand of what we call preservation crystals were deployed in deep caverns that it had been noted these primitives often frequented, leaving their marks.

We hoped that some future descendants of those hominids would find their way into the caverns at the estimated time of the star quakes, but we had hoped that if civilisation did take root that you would have spread out amongst the planets in your system thereby improving your chances of survival."

Scott interrupted.

"But we didn't. We'd only just started building bases on the moon. We were too busy trying to destroy each other."

"You are correct. It saddened us as we remained observing from a distance and our rules forbade us from too much direct interference. We had already done too much with the crystals.

The subsequent survival and rebirth of the human civilisation was not down to our efforts but to the amazing determination of your species to survive. None of the surviving pockets of humanity owed their existence to the crystals so we have been impressed with how over the last few thousand of your orbital cycles, the human species have hauled themselves, not just out away from the home planet but, to reach for the stars.

As Shalita will testify, there have been, in the last few of your cycles, small numbers who did emerge from their preservation, but the violence of the solar storms penetrated deeper than even we could have imagined and none of those survived to tell of what happened."

Shalita stirred at the mention of her name.

"So, what you are now admitting is that you knew all along about the crystals that Scott and Robyn had mentioned but only now have you informed us. The Terran council will not be pleased."

"True. However, it also means that Robyn and Scott are unique in being the only ones to have actually survived directly from your pre catastrophe era and as such we revere them. They are the only successes of the use of the crystals, but they were experimental and after deployment the project was terminated. We do understand that your time is limited but… "

Shalita cut Chel off suddenly. "He means that compared to the Alterans, we humans have a shorter life span. I believe our couple have heard enough for now and I know it must be overwhelming, so we shall take this up again in the next few days."

"Very well, I will be back in two of your described cycles and I look forward to continuing our conversation."

With that Chel and the four hosts took their leave as Robyn and Scott tried to take in what they had been told.

It was both mind blowing and a little disturbing...

"Your time is limited..?" echoed Robyn as she worriedly looked at Scott and he shrugged.

"May simply be a slip of the tongue and he did really mean we have different life cycles."

"I hope you are right, otherwise..." Robyn trailed off, not wanting to think that something more may be amiss with them.

It was a sobering thought...

CHAPTER 21: REVELATIONS II

Robyn had several days of feeling unwell and Scott became worried. They'd turned over one of the smart mobile phones to Dasheeda for the science community to analyse now that they had official access to its contents, but within a few days Robyn's poor health had begun. There was no connection, just random chance, but Shalita knew they now needed to inform the pair of their findings.

She met them in their new accommodation that had been provided in Beta base, as Theta was to become operational shortly and they had needed to be moved.

Word had spread about the unique humans and overall, they were welcomed into society as valued members, but it all seemed so alien now they knew that all along they had been preserved due to an alien race intervening...

The door chimed and Robyn passed her hand over the table in a specific way to open the door. They'd been allowed privacy, since early on. The three women and Paulo could in theory have entered without Scott or Robyn's approval but now they were a part of society, they were entitled to be more in control of their destiny.

The threesome sat down and a short while later Paolo also joined them.

"Are we honoured or what?" joked Robyn as Scott joined the group and sat with her, looking at them all facing the pair.

Shalita shuffled which was very odd, something they'd never seen her do before.

"We hope you are both settling in and enjoy the facilities Beta has to offer? I hope you have visited the halls of history as they have been updated with what you have told us and with the information your 'mobile phone' provided to our technicians. They have a lot to go on and I believe you'd say much of it was an eye opener." Shalita hoped this would settle the couple.

"We haven't been there yet but have explored the central gardens and talked to many people, it can be tiring at times, but they are all so friendly," answered Scott. "So, what is it? I mean the reason for this visit, you usually come along every five or six days."

"We have some news for you which is both good, and bad," offered Dasheeda and Shalita looked at her, frowning.

"We do have some information which we wanted to talk to you about on a personal level. It is of a delicate nature."

"The good news first then." Robyn felt she needed that after how she had felt over the last few days.

"Very well. As you know we are all constantly medically monitored and when we first rescued you there was an anomaly, but we needed more time to check it out.

Robyn, you are pregnant."

"Twins," added Dasheeda, not caring if Shalita disapproved of her blurting out the news.

Robyn sat open mouthed beside Scott as he shuffled closer to her in support, stunned and wondering if he was the father.

Carmalie anticipated the question. "We wondered a little about your relationship as, well this is a bit embarrassing, but from the devices you have allowed us to examine, the images of when you were not 'on holiday' showed each of you with another person?"

"Ahh, yes..." said Robyn slowly, still coming to terms with the news and figuring that was probably why she had been feeling unwell recently. "Our partners had secretly been seeing each other when we all joined up for our annual holiday together. Danny and Katrina preferred to sunbathe on the beaches whilst Scott and I shared a passion for exploration. But we, you know, Scott and me, we never did anything."

"Unlike Danny and Katrina who admitted everything when they were on their deathbeds. They had indeed been sleeping together in nearby hotels when we went off exploring the interior of the Algarve. We pretended that we had too so that they could die with their consciences clear." added Scott.

Carmalie looked intrigued. "That is interesting … the estimate for how long you have been pregnant for, is a strange figure, as you must have fallen pregnant before the catastrophe occurred and you became, shall we say, preserved in time." she started but Robyn jumped in.

"So, they must be Danny's…"

"No. The results are a match for you both." said Shalita.

"So, both Danny and Scott?" asked Robyn as Scott just sat there looking perplexed and Shalita continued.

"Again, no. The DNA results are of you and Scott, not this other male, your true partner, Danny."

Saying 'true partner' stung Robyn a little as she struggled to take all of it in.

Scott had remained quiet, but something clicked.

"Sam and Terry's party…" he said quietly, and Robyn looked at him open mouthed.

"Oh god, that drunken night…"

Scott turned to the others.

"Because Robyn and I were members of an explorer's club we sometimes had meetings at other member's houses sharing what we did during the holidays when we went exploring. But the night at Sam and Terry's was more of a celebration as it was the club's tenth anniversary and, well we got very drunk."

Scott looked at Robyn. "It's the only thing I can think of, and it was just a few weeks before we went out to the Algarve for our annual holiday.

Sam did tell me he found us in their spare bedroom passed out and in each other's arms on the floor so to spare us, he and Terry carried me to their room. If you remember we woke up in different rooms and as such thought nothing had happened."

Still shell shocked, Robyn kept shaking her head but had to admit that night was very hazy but there felt an inkling of truth at the back of her subconscious.

"We're going to have twins ..."

"We're going to have twins ..." echoed Scott and suddenly they were both standing up, jumping up and down holding each other's hands and laughing uncontrollably.

The others just sat and took in the spectacle until Shalita raised her hand and caught their attention.

Both sat back down and took deep breaths as they tried to calm down.

"Do you know their gender?" asked Robyn, now excited by the prospect.

"You wish to know?" replied Carmalie.

"YES!" came the joint reply from the prospective parents.

"Boy and girl. Healthy you will be pleased to know. We expect you to give birth in about seven and a third months from now, so naturally we will be monitoring you more closely Robyn to ensure both the twins and your health," explained Carmalie.

Scott looked at the four and cocked his head to one side then looked directly at Shalita.

"You said good *and* bad news at the start…"

Shalita pursed her lips. "As you know, we have been monitoring you carefully since you recovered and as we explained, you escaped the dire effects of the catastrophe due to being several hundred metres below the surface, unlike your original partners.

Despite that, I am saddened to have to tell you that we have detected a deterioration of your bodies that we cannot stop as we do not have the skills and neither do the best doctors of the GAA."

Robyn looked at her in horror. "But, how, how long have we got then?"

"It is not precise, but we have estimated that you will become seriously ill in about four or five years at the latest." Shalita watched this sink in.

Scott sat there looking dejected.

"Terminal?" he asked quietly.

The four looked down with sad faces, unable to meet their gaze.

"The twins …" muttered Robyn out loud.

"They appear to be perfectly healthy with none of the effects showing, but naturally we will be keeping a close watch on developments.

I…, we are very sorry to have to tell you the news, but we felt honesty was the best option. We are here for you no matter what happens."

Shalita turned to her three colleagues then back to the distraught couple. "Would you like us to leave?"

Robyn nodded as Scott looked at the foursome and stood.

"If you will please. We have a lot to think about."

Shalita again turned to the others and without any further words, they left Robyn and Scott as they hugged and cried together at the news.

CHAPTER 22: A LIMITED FUTURE...

Life, acceptance, and the birth of the twins changed things as Robyn and Scott began to raise Carrie and Harvey as they named the new arrivals. Paolo became Uncle Paulo along with Aunty Shalita and even from the age of two both children were quick to learn.

In the meantime, neither parent showed any signs of their impending demise and for a while life settled down to work, play and child minding. Work entailed often correcting the experts on how they had interpreted some of the information from the smart phones. There was a tendency to include extracts from novels or downloaded movies and TV shows as actual events so there were times when Robyn and Scott wondered just how advanced their hosts actually were.

At the age of three, the twins were allowed to accompany Scott and Robyn on a tour of the main bases of the solar system and as they drifted from planet to planet, it was a little difficult for the children to understand how emotional their parents were at seeing the giant planets in particular, close up in such detail.

It seemed growing up with information at their fingertips, Carrie and Harvey easily absorbed what was presented to them. It took a little longer for Robyn and Scott to keep up with the twin's progress.

They arrived back on the moon at Beta and happily settled back into their normal routines at their home until one day Shalita, Paolo, Carmalie and Dasheeda arrived as a group and asked to enter.

They sat down but Paolo looked at the other three and asked to take the twins into the adjacent room. Scott and Robyn knew something was wrong.

Shalita spoke.

"It has begun."

The looks on Robyn and Scott's faces said everything as their hearts sank with a reality check.

"How long?" Robyn didn't really want the answer, but they knew that for the twin's sake they had to face what was coming with dignity and fortitude.

"If the acceleration rate remains constant as it has for the last few weeks, then perhaps eighteen months to two years. Much as we originally suspected."

Scott looked thoughtful and then glanced at Robyn before addressing the three women.

"Then may we carry out our wish?"

"Yes, but the twins will not be able to accompany you even under these exceptional circumstances. Is that understood?" asked Shalita.

The couple nodded, holding hands and Robyn looked at the three in turn.

"Do you know what will happen?"

"Not fully but the rate of decline will accelerate in the final months. In some ways we expect it to be like ageing but on an incredible scale, but we can't be exact," offered Shalita as Carmalie nodded quietly in agreement.

"If you wish to undertake the tour then it must begin in the next few months. Any later and we can't guarantee that you won't deteriorate too much during it. We don't want that to happen if you are a long way away as it will take months to get back," she said.

"And the arrangements for the twins?" Robyn didn't like to ask but knew they had to make sure they would be looked after. She didn't need to worry as Shalita took her hand.

"Paolo and I will be looking after them. After all you have designated us as their uncle and aunt. They are used to us, and you may be surprised to know that they already suspect something is wrong with you both.

We have been careful not to reveal too much about where you came from, but naturally they are becoming very adept at using our resources, so my guess is that they probably actually know and are staying quiet for your sakes."

"We have provisional arrangements in place for you to leave on your tour in two months' time on the StarVista 4 cruiser. They have a great reputation, and their itinerary includes the major home worlds of the Galactic Arm Association. You will be welcomed as honoured guests and treated as VIPs; I think that is the correct term." added Dasheeda.

"We will be ready for your return, as will the twins," assured Shalita as they left so that Robyn and Scott could begin their own preparations for the eight-month voyage of a lifetime.

#

The voyage aboard the StarVista 4 had indeed been epic and emotional but now as Robyn and Scott, the celebrity VIPs, walked along the connecting tunnel they saw familiar figures ahead.

Shalita, Carmalie and Dasheeda had met them earlier then gone ahead to check things were in order, however, it was the sight of Paolo and the twins that gladdened Scott and Robyn's hearts.

Carrie and Harvey raced towards them but knowing how frail they were becoming they resisted the temptation to jump up into their arms or squeeze them too tightly.

"Missed you!" they both chimed which brought tears to Scott and Robyn's eyes. For all the wonders they had seen, seeing their twins was the most rewarding and heart-warming sight.

"So, have you two been good for Uncle Paolo and Aunty Shalita whilst we've been away?" asked Robyn as they reached the final checkout counter. The Alteran scanned everyone's biocode, smiled and waved them through where they were able to join Shalita, Carmalie and Dasheeda.

Carrie piped up. "Uncle Paolo is ace, can we stay with him and Aunty again next time?" she asked innocently, forgetting for a moment her parents would never be able to undertake another such trip. Harvey scowled at her and said nothing but just hugged Robyn then Scott in turn.

"They were very well behaved, and their learning is several leagues above the norm. You can be proud of them," Paolo said as he warmly and gently shook Scott's hand then lightly kissed Robyn on the cheek.

"Glad to hear it, but I think I speak for both of us when I say I'll be glad to get back home and see Earth again, even if it is from the moon, won't we Scott?"

"Indeed, we're pretty tired of all this travelling and need a rest to recover from this so-called holiday!" he answered with a weary smile.

The eight of them headed to another terminal as Shalita finalised the details and they boarded the smaller interstellar transport for the relatively short trip back to the solar system.

#

It was clear from the latest of many medical tests that they had arrived back just in time. Both were now beginning to look much older in a short space of time and it was clear the end was coming quicker than anyone wanted, least of all Robyn and Scott.

They were quietly terrified but had made a special request which needed formally ratifying from the Terran ruling council. Two days later back at Beta on the Moon, Carmalie and Dasheeda arrived to inform them of the result.

"No Shalita or Paolo?" asked Robyn in a quivering voice. Scott took her by the hand and looked into her eyes.

"Sweetheart, the twins are with them today. Today we find out if our wish will be granted," he said but then coughed into a small patch of linen that Carmalie had found for them. Their hosts had had no need for handkerchiefs for they couldn't remember how long ago it was when the resurgent human society had emerged, not requiring such things as handkerchiefs.

There was a little blood and Scott quickly squeezed the hanky into a ball and pushed it into his pocket.

"So?" he asked a little more pointedly than he'd intended.

"It is agreed. A rare situation but under the circumstances it was a united and universal result."

For the first time the couple saw tears welling up in their friends' eyes and Carmalie suddenly hugged Scott as Dasheeda did the same with Robyn.

The twosome immediately broke away and wiped the tears from their eyes.

"I am so sorry; it was unprofessional of us."

said Carmalie as Dasheeda too tried to wipe away the tears and regain her composure. Robyn looked at them both and smiled.

"Listen you two.

You were the first people I saw when I first began to wake up and you have stayed with us, caring for us, helping us to adjust, integrate and keep us as healthy as you could.

You are not just our hosts and medical staff, you are our trusted and dear to our hearts, *friends*."

Robyn gently hugged Dasheeda as they swapped over and Scott hugged Carmalie ever so gently.

"Have you been able to.." started Scott and Carmalie smiled through the tears.

"Yes. It seems that Paolo had thought of this eventuality right from the start and despite all the accommodation at Theta being allocated, he'd kept your original rooms on hold."

"When do we..?" A simple question but loaded with meaning as Robyn asked it.

"The transport will take us over tonight. How long do you want before…"

"I can feel things changing in real time, so it has to be tomorrow. The council's decision took longer than expected," said Carmalie. Robyn and Scott both now coughed and sat down heavily.

"Very well. I'll inform Shalita," replied Carmalie as calmly as she could before she and Dasheeda left.

EPILOGUE

They lay on the bed looking up at the large window that was the very same room and view screen from when they first arrived at Theta base.

The Earth still hung in the same place but was a little fuller in phase than how they remembered, but it didn't matter. Shalita brought the twins in and they each climbed up onto the bed, Harvey with Robyn and Carrie lying next to Scott as they in turn breathed heavily, laboured.

"The twins understand. They know what to do so just lie there and relax. The view is set to real view so no illusions, just as you asked." Carmalie and Dasheeda along with Paolo stepped into the room struggling to hide their emotions.

Shalita spoke for them all.

"We were there at the beginning and stand with you at the end. It has been a privilege and honour to have helped you these last few years and we will ensure the twins will never forget you and will bring you great honour. They will stay with you now and come to us when it is over.

The painkillers will help you on your final journey and we will always remember you with all our love and hearts.

Farewell dear friends."

The foursome left the room barely containing their grief as the twins snuggled in closer to their parents.

"Mother, we will remember you both, we will,

promise," said Harvey.

Scott's grip on Robyn's hand tightened a little at this.

"Yes darling, I'm sure you will. You be strong for us both and remember we will always love you." Robyn just got the words out before having a mild seizure, but she settled down as Harvey squeezed her hand gently.

"Daddy, we love you both and will see you again one day, I'm sure," said Carrie innocently, but Scott had begun to drift into a deep sleep. He stirred briefly and, holding Robyn's hand, he moved his head to look at her as she looked at him.

"Odd thing to pop into my head now but …

We never did get married, did we!" She said quietly.

He looked at her with a tear in his eye.

"It doesn't matter, that was a thing from a time long ago.

I love you Robyn."

"I love you too Scott …"

They lay back and went to sleep for the last time …

The End

AUTHORS NOTE

Many of the Sci Fi ideas for this novel and a few others planned have been brewing in my mind for a number of years. Sci Fi has usually been my main fiction reading material and some of the authors I have enjoyed over the years include Arthur C Clarke, Isaac Asimov, Edmund Cooper, A.E Van Vogt, and Alan Dean Foster. More recent authors have included the excellent Iain M. Banks, David Brin, Greg Bear and Stephen Baxter.

This novel has been heavily influenced by the many holidays Lorraine and I had in the Algarve when visiting COAA: Centre for Observational Astronomy in the Algarve run by the wonderful Bev and Jan Ewen-Smith.

The night sky was and is amazing from there and there are facilities for exploring it with telescopes, binoculars and getting your first taste of astrophotography.

Like Scott and Robyn in the novel, Lorraine and I enjoyed exploring the countryside and driving all over the region in search of butterflies, interesting natural sights and the scenery but unlike Scott and Robyn, we're happily married to each other!

Interestingly there is as small cave a few miles from there that I and my friend Nick along with two others did explore and that is the basis of this story but greatly exaggerated in its size and depth as you could barely get into it!

For some reason after visiting the caves I had the idea of a disaster story.

However, it was quite short so languished for quite a while until we heard the amazing story of the trapped Chilean Miners being saved in 2010. This brought the idea back to the fore but stayed low key until I had written 'The Fragility of Existence' in 2019 and several readers asked if there would be any more. So, Fragility of Survival' came into being.

Incidentally 'Carapaus Alimados' is a real, traditional, Algarvian dish although I've never tried it as I'm not a keen fan of fish!

Although the individual novels in the Fragility series are stories independent of each other, 'The Fragility of Survival' is definitely linked to the StarVista 4 saga and set in the same universe. Hence the voyage Robyn and Scott embark upon near the end is on the same space cruiser and set just a few years before the events begun in 'The Last Voyage of the StarVista 4'. So if you haven't read that book and its upcoming sequel then why not give the saga a read?

ASTROSPACE FICTION NEWSLETTER

To keep up to date with the novels written by Paul Money under the Astrospace Fiction banner, then why not sign up to the newsletter.

Those signing up will be the first to receive a *free* mini novel: "Lord Shabernackles of Grasceby Manor".

So, if you want to know more about the James Hansone Ghost Mysteries or the science fiction novels from Astrospace Fiction, such as how to purchase them and where, or when the next book in each series will be released, then simply sign up and you'll be the first to informed. There will also be occasional competitions or a give-away so worth subscribing to see what may be on offer soon. Note your information will not be passed on to third parties.

Just head on over to the following link where you can enter your email to be added to the newsletter list.

Note I will not share your email with anybody, and it is only for keeping up to date with Astrospace Fiction books.

https://mailchi.mp/1c69765ddf7a/jameshansonegm-signup

Best wishes and see you soon: Paul M

THE LAST VOYAGE OF THE STARVISTA 4

A Voyage of a lifetime.
2700 passengers and crew.
The diary of an eight-year-old passenger.
Stunning encounters with fabulous interstellar destinations.
The rings of the gas giant planet Tianca in the hardly explored Cantrara system.
A 100 year mystery in the making…

Follow the adventures of young Cherice Richmond, the youngest person allowed to undertake an eight-month star cruise on board the luxury star cruiser StarVista 4, with her parents, Carl and Natalie, the honourable newly appointed Earth Ambassadors to the Ziancan homeworld. Little do they know that they will never return…

Available on Amazon as Kindle, Paperback and Kindle Unlimited
Book 1 of a trilogy with Book 2: 'The Fate of the StarVista 4' coming soon.

THE JAMES HANSONE GHOST MYSTERIES

It all started with a simple unplanned diversion, 'A Ghostly Diversion'. James Hansone is a computer and IT specialist and a complete sceptic when it came to all things paranormal. Until that diversion. It changes everything once he becomes intrigued with a ghostly face at a broken window of a rundown cottage, deep in the Lincolnshire countryside. Little did he know that he would go on to uncover the mystery of a missing girl that would change his life forever.

Now with four sequels, James Hansone unwittingly becomes a ghost hunter roped in to explore further mysteries with more books planned in the series.

A Ghostly Diversion
Secrets of Grasceby Manor
Return to De Grasceby Manor
James and the Air of Tragedy
The Haunting of Grasceby Rectory
and coming soon: 'Spectre of the Grasceby Flier'
All available as kindle, print on demand and Kindle Unlimited from Amazon.

ABOUT THE AUTHOR

Paul L Money is an astronomy, writer, public speaker, publisher and occasional broadcaster. He is also the Reviews Editor for the BBC Sky at Night magazine and for eight years until 2013 he was one of three Astronomers on the Omega Holidays Northern Lights Flights.

He is married to Lorraine whose hobby/ interest is genealogy/ family history. As an astronomer Paul has been giving talks across the UK for over thirty years and was awarded the Eric Zuker award for services to astronomy in 2002 by the Federation of Astronomical Societies. In October 2012 he was awarded the 'Sir Arthur Clarke Lifetime Achievement Award, 2012' for his 'tireless promotion of astronomy and space to the public'. His first novels were ghost stories: 'A Ghostly Diversion' followed by the sequel, 'Secrets of Grasceby Manor', then 'Return to De Grasceby Manor' followed in 2019 with 'James and the Air of Tragedy' in 2020 and 'The Haunting of Grasceby Rectory in 2022 with 'Spectre of the Grasceby Flier' expected late 2023 and at least two more planned after that in the series.

A first foray into the realms of Sci Fi saw the publication of 'The Fragility of Existence' in early 2019, a version of the 'end of the world' stories that seem popular. 'Fragility of Survival' is a standalone novel with 2 more in the 'Fragility' series in development.

'The *Last* Voyage of the StarVista 4' is the first novel to take place in the Galactic Arm Association (GAA) Universe, published in 2021 and several more are planned, one 'The Fate of the StarVista 4' will be a sequel due mid-2023, whilst a third (The Legacy of the StarVista 4) will follow in due course. Another novel almost fully written (*'This New Horizon'*) will be the first of another trilogy whose story will eventually link up with the saga begun with 'The *Last* Voyage of StarVista 4'.

More info can be found at the Astrospace web site:
Astrospace/ Astrospace publications
http://www.astrospace.co.uk

Check out Paul's Amazon author page:
https://www.amazon.co.uk/Paul-L.-Money/e/B003VNGE1M

August 2023

Printed in Great Britain
by Amazon